SHELLSHOCKED

BOOK TWO

SAN DIEGO PARANORMAL POLICE DEPARTMENT

JOHN P. LOGSDON

JENN MITCHELL

CRIMSON MYTH
PRESS

Published by: Crimson Myth Press (www.CrimsonMyth.com)

Thanks to TEAM ASS!
Advanced Story Squad

This team is my secret weapon. Their job is to help me keep things in check and also to make sure I'm not doing anything way off base in the various story locations!

(listed in alphabetical order by first name)

Audrey Cienki
Bennah Phelps
Carolyn Fielding
Cindy Deporter
Emma Porter
Hal Bass
Helen Day
Janine Corcoran
Julie Peckett
Karen Hollyhead
Kathleen Portig
Larry Diaz Tushman
Leslie Watts
Malcolm Robertson
Marcia Lynn Campbell
Mary Letton
Melony Power
Michelle Reopel
Myles Mary Cohen
Nat Fallon
Paige Guido

Penny Noble
Sandee Lloyd
Scott Reid
Sharon Harradine
Terri Adkisson

CHAPTER 1

Jin

Guns don't kill people. *I* kill people.

— JIN KANNON

Everyone was standing around the main conference room table going through what they knew about Emiliano, the zombies, and the new drug known as *Shaded Past #13*. Unfortunately, they didn't know much. Jin expected Hector, or at least his goons, to have the most to offer, but they'd described Emiliano as being "secretive as hell, ruthlessly violent when pushed about his secrets, and in constant need of having his ego stroked…among other things."

Jin chose not to ask what "among other things" referred to, recognizing enough about this group already to know that'd be a bad idea.

Just when he was about to start pushing everyone to

come to a conclusion about the group's plan, Rusty called out over the speakers in the room.

"Hey…boss."

Everyone went quiet and looked over at Jin. He, on the other hand, found himself looking at Miss Kane, since he'd been told about the Mistress/submissive relationship the precinct's succubus tech chief had with the squad's A.I.

Miss Kane shook her head. "He's not talking to me, Chief Kannon. Rusty knows better than to use such lowly titles with me, and he would never use that tone of voice. Isn't that right, my little naughty collection of zeroes and ones?"

"I would never refer to you in such a way, Mistress!"

"Right," Jin said, unable to hide the disturbing feelings he felt in that moment. Miss Kane merely leaned back against the wall, crossed her arms, and gave him a deadpan look. "Um, what is it that you want, Rusty?"

"Deep question. I don't know. The same things as any good submissive, I suppose. Someone superior to call me names, ridicule me, delete little portions of my code here and there, and maybe send a shock across my motherboard now and then."

Now everyone in the room was finding it difficult to hide their disturbed feelings.

As for Miss Kane, she appeared to be enjoying their discomfort. When Jin glanced at her after Rusty's admission, she was smirking something fierce, and it wasn't a pleasant smirk either.

"I'm asking why you called out to me over the loudspeaker, Rusty."

"Well, when I get all riled up, I sometimes—"

"Rusty? Why did you call me over the speaker?"

"The reason I called...boss, was to tell you I'm getting flooded with reports about massive zombies rolling over the city. People are getting wiped out, snatched away, and so on."

The lights in the room dimmed and the wall filled with what Jin assumed was a video feed from the city.

"I pulled up the cameras in the area and you can definitely see there's trouble...boss."

Indeed there was, which was difficult to focus on with Rusty speaking to him in such a way, but he chose to mostly ignore it.

Bodies were flying left and right as the zombies tore through a crowd of people. While there was no sound to accompany the video, it didn't take a genius to know there was a lot of screaming going on. Those zombies were strong and ferocious.

One of the more interesting aspects was watching as the zombies climbed walls or poles and smacked out the cameras that were surveilling them.

Seconds later, the feed they were watching went to static.

"We've got to get down there fast!" Raina called out, rushing from the room as everyone else followed suit after her.

The only two left standing were Jin and Miss Kane.

"You have an interesting relationship with Rusty, Miss Kane."

"It's *Mistress* Kane," Rusty corrected him from above.

"Not to me, it isn't," he replied, tipping his hat at the succubus. She raised an eyebrow at him. "Not to me."

He walked out of the room and found everyone gearing up. They hadn't done so when they were heading to Hector's house to liberate Director Fysh, but it was clear this was a different kind of threat. His team had experienced firsthand what it was like to engage with the zombies. The power behind those monsters was evident. Apparently, the rapport between the PPD and *The Dogs* was such that they never felt the need to fully gear up. Jin found that strange, but there wasn't much about his crew he'd found normal thus far.

Raina followed him into his office and walked over to the steel cabinet to the right of the room. She opened it up, revealing a set of gear that was apparently built for the chief. Unfortunately, it was clear this particular set had been designed for Director Fysh.

"It's not going to fit perfectly, chief," Raina said, dragging the suit out, "but it's better than nothing."

"I think I'll make do with what I have already, Raina, but thanks."

"That's not smart!...um...chief."

"She's right," Miss Kane said as she walked in and held up a device that cast a series of blue lines all over Jin. He jolted. "Stay still, you big baby. It's not going to hurt you. I'm getting your measurements." She paused her scan for a moment, focusing on his groin region. "Nice." He grimaced at her, but she ignored it and finished the scan. "All set. Rusty, you toadish little worm, I've sent you Chief Kannon's measurements. Animate his suit immediately."

"Of course, Mistress."

Miss Kane reached out and pulled Raina away from the locker, taking Director Fysh's outfit away from her. "I'll make sure she gets this."

"Thanks," said Raina.

A new suit formed as they watched. It was a bit different than the one Raina was wearing, and much different than the one Miss Kane was currently holding. This one was thin, almost like a set of tight-fitting pajamas. It was black with blue striping and there was a small San Diego PPD logo on the upper-right of the chest.

"That's going to protect him?" asked Raina.

Miss Kane laughed. "It's my latest technology. I know it doesn't look as sturdy as the outfit you have on, but I assure you it's three times as strong, not to mention much easier to move around in." She glanced over at Jin. "Also, note that it's got moisture control so it'll keep you nice and cool, and it'll show off your bulges, too."

"Any chance we can get suits like that, too?"

"Yes, Raina," answered Miss Kane, "but not yet. This one needs to be tested in the field first."

Great, so Jin was a guinea pig. Not ideal, but considering the fact that he was planning to go without a suit entirely made it unimportant anyway.

"I'd honestly rather just go as I am," he stated.

"Sorry, chief," Raina said, shaking her head, "precinct rules. Chief...erm...Director Fysh put that into practice a couple of years back. Everyone on the force has to wear them whenever we're facing a big threat."

"But none of you wore them when we went to Hector's house," argued Jin.

Raina seemed confused by that. "That's because *The*

Dogs aren't a big threat unless we're in a war with them. They'd just kidnapped the chief...Director. Well, she was the chief when they kidnapped her, anyway."

He was going to argue the point, but would it even matter? No.

"Fine," he said, waving at them to leave the office. "I'll put the damn thing on. Have everyone ready to leave in five minutes. We need to get downtown pronto!" That's when he noticed the only people still standing in the main bullpen were Raffy, Petey, Hector, Sofia, Cano, and Alejandro. "They're already gone?"

"No offense, chief," Raina replied somewhat pensively, "but they weren't going to sit around waiting for you to get yourself together. Like you said, getting to the city center fast is the priority."

"Right."

Jin sighed and shooed them out of his office, noting all the while that Miss Kane was simply delighting in the chaos. She may have claimed to no longer feel the pull of the stereotype that surrounded being a succubus, but it sure didn't look that way.

After shutting the door and closing the blinds, Jin started stripping out of his outfit to put his new protective garb on under it.

"You can take the woman out of the succubus, but you can't take the succubus out of the woman," he whispered, before frowning at himself. "Well, that sounded wrong."

CHAPTER 2

Vestin

*H*e was pleased with the new recruits for his army. The numbers weren't quite there yet, but at least there was progress. With the Comic-Con event looming, the crowds in San Diego were growing, and soon Vestin's army would be teeming with bodies.

"And you're certain the brand of normals who will be attending this conference will suit our needs, Prender?"

"Most definitely, My Lord," Prender replied, fancying the new medal that Vestin had affixed to his jacket moments earlier.

Vestin understood that people like Prender needed a morale boost now and then. Without it, they tended to flounder. While Prender wasn't as proud and ego-driven as Emiliano, he still needed the occasional kudos in order to keep him happy. Vestin couldn't allow anyone to become lax in their duties. At some point, he would do away with his second-in-command, and probably

Emiliano—the jury was still out on that decision—but it wouldn't be for a while yet. For now, he needed Prender in order to keep all his plans on track, and he needed Emiliano to keep his particular style of recruitment going.

Vestin would have preferred relying only on himself, of course, but he was wise enough to recognize that even a king needed the aid of his servants. Delegation was the key to success in almost any venture. The trick was finding people who would do as they were told without finding it in themselves to seek greater glory unless said glory was sufficiently represented by a new jingling decoration on their uniform.

Prender was easy; Emiliano, not so much.

"Where is our head zombie?"

"He's attacking the city, My Lord," Prender replied smartly. "Sorry, I mean he's 'gathering recruits.'"

That was somewhat concerning. It showed a lack of foresight since a swarm of zombies running around in a crowded city, taking lives, kidnapping, and the like was bound to cause a touch of panic. That, in turn, could result in fewer people showing up for the conference.

"Prender," Vestin said, his voice calm, "are you certain it's wise for him to attack people prior to the event?"

Prender looked suddenly worried. "My Lord?"

"Would it not be more wise to wait for the full contingent of travelers to arrive before spooking everyone from arriving at all?"

"Oh, uh…well…"

Vestin held out his hand, giving Prender a disappointed gaze. In response, his second-in-command slowly removed the new medal he'd been admiring. He then stepped over and gingerly placed it in Vestin's hand.

The look on the man's face was enough to stroke Vestin's own ego.

"When you learn to think a little more critically, Prender, you may have this back." He opened the little drawer on the side of his fancy throne and dropped the medal unceremoniously inside. "Until then, I would suggest you find a way to get through to Emiliano and make sure he doesn't cause too much destruction." His eyes locked firmly on Prender's. "I would hate to remove even more of your precious medallions."

The worry in Prender's eyes was intense. Funny how the threat of bodily harm wasn't nearly as effective against a man like him.

"I'll take care of it straightaway, My Lord!"

With that, Prender rushed from the room, leaving Vestin alone with Carina.

The witch was shaking her head at Vestin. He wasn't pleased with such a reproach from the woman, especially since he barely knew her. There was little he could do, though. She was un-bite-able, at least for the moment. He would need her magic soon and it'd been made clear to him that any attempt to introduce his venom would result in her inability to comply. Oh, she'd *want* to comply because she'd be under his rule, but there were seemingly limitations to what even Vestin's newfound concoction was capable of managing. To be fair, he wasn't one hundred percent certain she'd lose her magic since his venom *was* different than the average vampire's. He just wasn't willing to risk the possibility at this time.

Fortunately, Carina wasn't like Prender. Bodily harm *did* seem to play a factor in her willingness to help.

"Is there something you wish to say, witch?"

She sniffed. "Your second-in-command is weak, not to mention visibly dense. I'm honestly surprised Emiliano would follow someone who chooses generals so poorly."

Vestin's eye twitched.

"I would use caution when speaking to me in such a way. While I currently accept that my venom may well hinder your magic, I'm not above seeing how effective a whip may be in improving your attitude."

Carina swallowed hard, her judging look turning to one of concern.

The key to being an effective overlord was something vampires taught their younglings from day one. Vestin still had the index card stowed away in his personal chest of memorabilia, though he had committed them to memory years ago.

- *A vampire must always look the part.*
- *A vampire must seek the pain points of each minion and press upon them wisely.*
- *A vampire must feed cautiously, only spreading venom where the spread will prove beneficial.*

There were many more, of course. It came with the territory of being the ultimate race in the Netherworld— and topside. But the rest had more to do with the proper use of hair gels, tooth-filing techniques, and the most effective methods of using brooding stares.

"Were I you, witch, I should find myself spending

more of my time thinking about how I may effectively tap into dark energy when called upon to do so." He leaned back in his chair and crossed his legs. "Do note that I'm rarely forgiving. When I command something to be done, I expect results. Failure to provide them, or any discourse that I deem insulting or disobedient, will be met with a dire response." His face softened. "There won't be enough pain to result in making you incapable of doing your work, however. I'm not a monster. You'll experience just enough discomfort to ensure you'll not wish to challenge me again. If you do, I shall increase the level of pain until we find your breaking point. Once we learn your limits, you'll find the greatest anguish will be the anticipation of the next cycle of discipline."

She was as pale as the moon at that moment.

"Do we have an understanding, witch?"

In response, she nodded at him slowly.

"I'm sorry, I couldn't hear you." He folded his hands together. "Do we or do we not have an understanding?"

The rasp was barely audible. "We do."

"We do what?"

"Have an understanding."

"No, I mean…" Vestin let out an annoyed breath. "You need to refer to me as 'My Lord,' Carina. Seriously. Have you not been listening to everyone else?"

She frowned at him, something in her eyes saying that he was acting rather like a child.

"Um, sorry. We have an understanding, My Lord."

CHAPTER 3

Jin

Jin was glad Raina knew where she was going because he would have been completely lost. Most of the roads appeared to be in a grid pattern, so it's not like he couldn't have sorted it out eventually, but he'd read somewhere that you needed to live in a place for a least a year before you started to feel comfortable with how to get around. With Jin being barely one day in, he was decidedly *not* comfortable yet.

"Where are we going exactly?" he asked.

She pointed at the screen on the dashboard. "Rusty mapped it out as the attacks being focused primarily on Gallagher Square."

"Any reason why?"

"I suppose that's where the reports centered," she answered. "You see, there are a lot of supers living up here who act kind of like a neighborhood watch where—"

"Sorry, Raina, I meant can you imagine any reason why the zombies would attack that location?"

"Oh! The only thing I can think of is that it'll be loaded with people." She gave him a quick glance. "It's a park, chief, and there are a bunch of people flowing into the city right now because of the upcoming Comic-Con and we usually see a number of them show up at the park."

Comic-Con was something he'd read about, though only briefly. As far as he could remember it was a conference for people who were into comics, science fiction and fantasy movies and books, and things like that. If memory served, some attendees dressed up in interesting costumes and got into a bit of roleplaying.

Looking down at his own outfit told him he may actually fit in with the crowd.

Whatever. Jin wasn't about to change the way he dressed, at least not without taking a bit of time to get used to the idea. His crew wore mostly regular clothes, though they were currently donning full gear due to the impending confrontation. Director Fysh had been dressed a little nicer than the rest of the squad. Was Jin supposed to do the same? If so, that was going to be yet another check in the "minuses" column on his mental pluses/minuses sheet regarding staying aboard with the PPD.

They turned onto J Street.

"It's up on the left here," Raina said.

She hadn't needed to say a word, because with all the people running away from the spot it was pretty obvious. His officers were already on the scene and they were engaged in battle. Hector and his crew had gone off to check on their various properties, which was for the best since Jin was still coming to grips with the PPD working alongside the cartel. Raffy and Petey stayed back at the precinct.

Raina sped up to the crosswalk and slid the car to an angled stop, clearly making sure no other vehicles would be able to get through while also making sure she didn't hit anybody.

Jin jumped out of the car first this time. He grabbed his guns and ran at full speed toward the battle.

It wasn't his norm to fight this way, but he wanted to make sure everyone knew he wasn't the guy they'd seen at Hector's place during their last encounter with the zombies. Jin—the *real* Jin—had returned to his normal self and he wasn't going to freeze up again. His only problem was that he'd been used to working a certain way, which included doing a fair bit of reconnaissance before engaging. He wanted to know the layout of a place, the entrances, the exits, and the hidden escape routes. Since they were at a park, those answers were obvious.

Just as he reached the first patch of grass, a body flew over him and landed with a crunching thud. He slid on his heels and glanced back to make sure it wasn't one of his own. It wasn't, but what he saw didn't provide much relief. Looking down at the broken body of a young woman lying there left little doubt the integration hadn't been reversed when it came to Jin's desire to protect normals.

His ire increased.

Spinning back, Jin found himself about twenty feet away from the zombie who had just annihilated the poor woman on the ground. The thing looked rather pleased with himself, too.

Four rapidly-fired bullets later, each placing an equal number of holes through the beast's skull, it dropped to the ground.

"Wow, chief!" Raina said as she rushed by. "That was amazing!"

There'd been no time to reply. Not that he would have. In Jin's estimation, the only people who should ever be impressed with a person's ability to kill are those who hire people with a penchant for killing, and even then it should be noted that those people were just as sick as the people they hired.

He shook his head and frowned, recognizing he was thinking that way about himself.

"If the shoe fits, Jin," he whispered before shooting down another zombie.

Once he got to the thick of the fight, he found his squad was battling ferociously.

Lacey was casting spells to blind the creatures, or at least that's what Jin assumed since they were grabbing at their eyes and running around haphazardly. The moment she had one dazed and confused, she'd blast it with fireballs, causing it to run face-first into a tree or wall. Even better was when she guided them to smack into one of their own kind. She had two of them beating the hell out of each other, making it obvious they had no idea who they were even fighting.

Chimi stood toe-to-toe with a larger zombie, trading blows with the damn thing. Neither one of them seemed to be getting ahead of the other, but the power of their punches was loud enough to sound like shotgun blasts. Jin helped her out by placing a bullet directly between the zombie's eyes. Chimi's final punch knocked the monster flat on its ass before she jumped up and brought both feet down on its chest.

The resulting crunch was not something Jin would soon forget.

Rudy had his gun trained on one of them and was blasting away. He would never have been given a job with the Assassins' Guild, but he handled the weapon well enough to be a cop in the PPD. Rudy didn't need perfect shooting skills anyway, but that's only because Clive had taken to using his magical tail, wrapping it around a zombie to hold it in place. Once that one hit the ground, he snaked his tail to clothesline another who was trying to get to his partner.

Jin had seen a fair number of strange things in his day, but Clive's tail was something new altogether.

Brrrrrrrt!

He knew that sound immediately. It was Raina's M134 and it was lighting up the zombies near her, turning them into a fine red mist.

"*Be careful with that thing!*" Rudy bellowed through the connector. "*There are a lot of normals here, you know?*"

"*I'm not the one who scored dead last in marksmanship, Rudy,*" Raina shot back. "*Unlike you, I don't miss!*"

"*I don't miss either!*"

"*That's after bein' bullshit,*" Lacey laughed. "*If it wasn't fer yer magically-gifted horsey, the only thing ye'd hit would be air!*"

"*Hey,*" Clive chimed in, "*leave me out of this!*"

Normals were darting all over the place, doing their best to escape the mayhem. It was the only thing that was helping to keep Jin from going completely batshit. He hated that they were being put in this situation at all, but to see they were at least smart enough to recognize it wasn't some crazy gimmick for the upcoming show made him able to control the power of his integration.

"Shit!"

That was Clive. He'd been tackled by a zombie, leaving Rudy in the precarious position of proving he could hit more than air when shooting.

He couldn't.

The most recent zombie he'd been trying to hit bobbed and weaved until it launched itself through the air, cannoning into the much smaller man. It might have been worse, of course. Rudy could've panicked and morphed into a rooster.

Another yelp drew Jin's attention to focus on Raina, who had just been rushed from behind, losing control of her weapon. It clattered to the ground as she did her best to fight the beast clawing at her outfit. Jin winced at the sight, hoping he was more concerned for Raina than the M134.

Again, he shook his head at himself.

"Ow!" shrieked Lacey an instant after that. It seemed one of the zombies had reached up and batted her out of the sky. That would've been bad enough, but what made it worse was how she'd bounced off Chimi's face, her miniature magic wand poking directly into the cyclops' massive eye.

"Argh!"

His entire team was laid out, or in the process of being laid out, anyway. It was time to save their asses.

Like a cowboy from the Old West of the Badlands, Jin steeled himself, snarled and focused, and then let his guns rip. Within seconds, each member of his crew was free of the zombies that had previously gotten the better of them. His aim was true, as it always was, and he wasted no time on being pretty about it.

A skull filled with lead was a skull that held no life, even zombie "life."

"Holy shit, chief," Rudy said, getting back to his feet and brushing himself off. *"I guess that means they really* did *put the real you back in that head of yours, eh?"*

Jin gave him a grim look. *"We're not done here, Captain."*

"Actually, chief," Raina corrected him, *"the zombies are taking off, so it looks like we are done."*

"Oh."

He watched for a few moments to make sure the zombies were indeed fleeing the area. It could've been that they were just going to find another place to spread havoc, but if that happened Rusty would tell them. Right?

"Rusty," he called back to the station, *"keep us posted if there are more attacks. We've cleared out the park but we're not sure if the zombies are done or not."*

"Whatever you say, chief."

The tone of Rusty's response gave Jin pause. *"Is there something wrong, Rusty?"*

"Other than you trying to make time with my Mistress? No, nothing at all...chief."

Oh boy. If it wasn't one thing, it was another.

"I wasn't trying to make time with anyone, Rusty. We merely had a conversation and nothing more."

Not exactly true, and why the hell was he explaining himself to an AI anyway?

"Whatever you say...chief."

Jin decided to stay on target and he wanted to make sure his dispatcher did the same. "Stay professional, Rusty. That's an order. Got it?"

"I'm always professional...chief."

Jin shook his head and put his guns back in their holsters before going to help one of the normals who was slowly coming back to consciousness.

"What happened?" the guy asked as he rubbed his eyes.

"Well, uh," Jin began and then stopped himself. "Uh, well, you see...there were...um..."

Raina grabbed him by the arm and started dragging him away. "We don't talk to the normals about the crazy things, chief. That's a big no-no." She then got on her connector. "Rusty, get The Cleaners down to Gallagher Square pronto. We've got a lot of normals injured and many more who are freaking out."

"They're on their way!"

He sounded chipper and cheery when responding to her. Of course, he did. She hadn't had "a conversation" with Miss Kane.

Ugh.

"Sorry, The Cleaners?" Jin asked.

Raina looked about to respond, but after a few false starts, she merely shrugged and said, "You'll see, chief. You'll see."

CHAPTER 4

Hector

He was hoping to find more unturned *Dogs* around the various compounds, but so far they were all zombies. Most of them he couldn't recognize, but now and then he, or one of his henchmen, would spot someone they knew and the pieces would fall into place. The zombie look was just so different. They were all quite tall, had cracked or holed flesh, were missing some or all of their teeth, and so on. It was a very bad look, so Hector couldn't fault himself for finding it difficult to spot people he'd spent a lifetime with. Hell, even his father was unrecognizable to him when they'd had their first run-in with the zombies.

It was still odd to Hector that Carina had recognized his father immediately, but based on how Sofia, Cano, and Alejandro were picking out members of the *Dogs* like nothing had changed about them at all told Hector *he* was the one who was the anomaly.

"How are you all doing that?" he asked.

Sofia gave him a funny look. "Doing what?"

They were standing at one of the entrances to a tunnel, just inside the shaded part where they couldn't be seen. It was Surveillance 101. That was according to Sofia, anyway.

"You're pointing at different zombies and naming them like they haven't changed in the slightest."

Cano chuckled. "That's because we know how they all move, boss."

"Yep," agreed Alejandro. "When you're a fighter—no offense—you study a few things." He glanced back out toward the field. "The look in a person's eye, the way they carry themselves, how close they keep their arms in when they walk, how fast they shuffle, what their head does when they're out and about. Are they looking straight head, do they constantly check over their shoulder, or maybe they have their head on a swivel?"

"Exactly," Sofia agreed. "You have to know all the ins and outs of a person so you can judge how best to fight them, or how to best utilize them in a fight against a rival gang."

Hector hadn't known anything about any of that. Yes, he'd been in a number of fights over his time. It was a requirement of being a *Dog*, even if you were the son of the head honcho. Emiliano had barely given Hector any real rearing when it came to battle, though, considering the boy soft and impure.

Was it Hector's fault Emiliano had slept with a normal and caused said impurity? No. But damn if you wouldn't think it was.

All his life, Emiliano merely grumbled at him, called him weak, and "tolerated" him. Now and then he'd show minor interest, but even when those rare instances occurred they most often ended up with Hector being on the short end of some terrible adventure as Emiliano shook his head in disappointment.

The henchmen all got training, entertainment, drinks with the boss, and were even allowed in on top secret meetings…some were, at least.

That was not the case with Hector.

For him, existence was just one boring day after another, each a reminder that he was an unwanted piece of his father's life. As he aged, Hector tried his best to force his way into the business, bringing new ideas to the table that he truly believed would improve things for everyone. Emiliano despised his son's plans, though, stating, "I can't believe I've underestimated just how weak you are, boy."

Kindness was not a skill Emiliano had bothered to cultivate during his life, which likely explained why it was one Hector sought every step of the way. He'd not only wanted to distance himself from Emiliano, he had wanted to be the antithesis of the man.

And now that he was the boss of *The Dogs* he was going to do his damndest to make that happen. That'd been the plan until the whole zombie thing happened, at least.

The only thing that made any sense about the entire ordeal was how Emiliano had somehow come back from the dead to yet again take over and rub Hector's nose in the shit. Even in death, his father remained a complete asshole. Hector shouldn't have been surprised by that, considering who he was talking about, but to have zero reprieve was irritating him more and more as each second slipped by.

Hector had finally been given the chance to do something with his life and he would be damned if his dead father was going to screw that up.

He just didn't know what exactly he could do about it.

Emiliano was far more powerful now than he'd ever been, and the soldiers he'd collected in this new army of his nearly equaled his power. They were loyal, too. Hell, Hector couldn't help but imagine Sofia, Cano, and Alejandro—especially Alejandro—were probably thinking how they wouldn't mind stepping out into the open and getting chomped on until they were turned, all so they could regain their regular positions under their old boss.

Part of him wanted to ask them if they'd prefer to just go out and do just that.

That's when he noticed Sofia was staring at him.

"What?" he asked.

"I know what you're thinking," she replied, "and I'd be lying if I said I hadn't considered it, but no. The bottom line is Emiliano ain't what he was before. Oh, he's still an asshole, but this is an entirely new kind of asshole we're dealing with now." She glanced back outside. "Falling into that shit holds no honor at all."

Honor?

"I agree," said Cano. "Besides, I kind of like the direction you're wanting to take *The Dogs*, boss. Having a community…a family? That's nice."

To his shock, Alejandro was nodding sagely.

He sighed at seeing the look on Hector's face.

"You already know I think you're weak," the man said. "You barely know how to fight, you smell like a flower most of the time, and your know-it-all, better-than-everyone attitude makes me want to kick you in the neck." He groaned and rolled his eyes. "But dammit, these two idiots are right. I may be violent, but being a zombie takes it to a level even *I* think is too far. They have no code, no honor." He glanced at the others before giving Hector a serious stare. "Plus, the community thing is good. It's something Emiliano should have seen, had he been able to see it."

Hector was floored. He had no clue how to respond to any of them, other than to double down on his desire to win this damn thing and get *The Dogs—his Dogs—*rolling in the way he knew they should be.

"I appreciate it, gang," he said, but kept his voice strong. "If we're going to make that happen, though, we're going to need to get back to the PPD and work with them." Their shoulders slumped slightly. "Do any of you see another option? If you do, I'm open to any and all suggestions." He held up a finger. "And don't even suggest I contact Mr. Becerra, since we all know damn well he won't risk sending more members of the cartel to fall under the zombie collective my father is building."

After a few shared glances, they collectively shook their heads to show they had no other ideas.

"Me neither, and it's the *only* reason I'm willing to work with the police on this."

That wasn't true. Frannie Fysh was still the light of his life, even though he'd tried like mad to hide it from himself since they'd broken up. The looks on his team's faces told him they again knew what he was thinking.

"Yeah, okay, so I still have feelings for Chief Fysh."

"She's a Director now, remember?" Sofia teased.

"True." That made things even more difficult. The head of *The Dogs* pairing up with a Director in the PPD? No way that could happen. "True."

After one last glance outside, Hector turned and started back into the tunnels.

"Let's get going and see what we can do to help get *our* city back!"

CHAPTER 5

Mistress Madison Kane

There was something about the new chief that interested her. She couldn't quite place it, but there was definitely an allure. Toughness? Possibly, though she'd known many tough people in her life. Assassin-tough, however? That *was* new, and it was a challenge.

The default position her mind was taking regarding the man was that he was a challenge, at least. But was that really what drove her interest?

No.

Their conversation on the beach was what captured her.

Jin Kannon was an ex-assassin who wanted nothing more than to spend the rest of his life *not* being an assassin. He longed for peace and tranquility. He longed to find a new truth that lasted to his final breath.

In other words, he was the male counterpart to Madison herself.

Being a succubus is a delicious way to live, at first. After decades of experiencing every possible debauchery she could imagine—and quite a few more she never would've imagined without the assistance of minds even more warped than her own—it had become a mundane existence. Deviances that were once wonderful diversions had become just another day on the job. For a long time after she'd lost interest in those particular activities, Madison found minor solace in the kick she still got out of conquering people who were powerful, even if only in their own minds. Breaking a person is luscious to a succubus. Sadly, she'd lost the taste for it.

Then she found technology. It was a different kind of challenge. She couldn't use standard manipulation tactics in order to get things to go her way. She had to study, struggle, push the boundaries of her own mind, and rage at the various facets of code and machine in order to bend it to her will. Finally, after a number of years of dedicated effort, she began seeing marked improvement in her skills.

She started hacking soon after, finding a new medium of manipulating people through data, and she was able to do it in vast numbers. That had quickly become her new passion.

Too bad she'd been caught sniffing around the wrong server complex.

It'd been a trap and a damn good one at that.

Utilizing bait that only someone of her kind would find appealing, they'd lured her in slowly...oh so slowly.

She'd get so far, and then have the prize ripped away, inches from her grasping fingers. It was tantalizing and thrilling, eating every waking moment of her days and nights. With every two steps she'd taken forward in her hack, she'd fall back another three as yet new encryptions and virtual doors blocked her way. Honestly, it was better than sex. Unfortunately, to a succubus, that kind of teasing eventually led to carelessness. Her pursuit ceased being about a careful hack and instead became about winning.

In other words, Madison lost control and became reckless enough to get busted.

Nancy Rendson, the woman who had masterminded the entire trap, was a normal with the genius of a succubus, at least when it came to computers and technology. Her deft use of tantalizing crumbs had brought Madison in and trapped her, nailing her to the circuit board and giving her quite the spanking in the process, in a manner of speaking.

So it came as a complete shock to learn that Nancy had lobbied to have Madison brought into the Paranormal Police Department. The woman clearly recognized the succubus had mad skills, assuming they were contained. Madison accepted the option without hesitation. Not doing so would have left her in a confined space for years. Succubi were fine playing games in small areas, but incarceration was *not* a game.

Soon after taking the job, Madison pursued Nancy and then dated her for roughly a year. It wasn't a pursuit of interest beyond knowing the woman had bested her. That was a no-no to a succubus, and so *Mistress* Madison

Kane systematically broke Nancy down, little by little, but soon saw what she was doing and stopped before it was too late.

Madison stopped the entire "Mistress" crap with her, recognizing she just couldn't take it any further.

Nancy was far too intelligent. She was fantastic at her job, and she was cunning. To break her would be to remove that ability, forcing the woman's mind into wanting nothing more than to serve Mistress Kane's every desire. The respect she'd gained for Nancy's abilities disallowed her to continue.

Madison simply couldn't do it, and that was very odd indeed.

The day she removed her tentacles from Nancy was the day Madison recognized that she could no longer act as a pure succubus. She'd lost her mojo, finding something much more compelling along the way. She still played the games, finding it difficult to completely divorce herself from who she was at her core, but that's all they were to her now: games. And they *were* still fun, as long as she took care to avoid them becoming more serious.

But now she was finding herself thinking of the new chief of the PPD, and not in a "games" way, either. Well, maybe a little of that. It wasn't the focus, though. She also wasn't looking at him through the lenses of a succubus. What she *was* feeling was genuine interest in another soul who seemed to be as lost as she was.

Madison, much to her own surprise, was considering a true relationship.

She shook her head and turned the corner to walk into her office.

That's when she saw the Stinkfoot and the fallen angel, and they were tinkering around with items on her main workbench.

"What the hell are you two doing?" she asked. "I don't recall asking you to come to my office and touch anything."

"I tried to tell them, Mistress, but—"

"Silence!"

Okay, Mistress Kane *had* enhanced Rusty's coding so he'd become the perfect submissive, but since it'd been done using zeroes and ones and not through a long, drawn-out process of manipulation, she felt okay with it. He was useful and he gave her mental—and often physical, via "items" she'd invented for such purposes—stimulation when she required it of him.

"Now, again," Madison said, her arms crossed as she stared at the two idiots who hadn't seemed all that bothered by her attitude, "why are you messing around in my office?"

"You're doing this wrong," Petey replied, holding up a weapon. "I'm fixing it."

It was the new M134-style designed mini-gun she'd been working on for weeks. Her goal had been to take the beast Raina used now and then and make a hand-held version of it. She'd sorted it out for the most part, including building miniature breaker bullets that contained various fragments like wood and silver to make sure they were effective when used against the various supernatural races. Her biggest issue was that the damn thing kept seizing up when it got hot.

"Fixing it?" she said, reaching out to snake it away from Petey. She looked it over carefully, hoping he hadn't broken anything. "What do you mean fixing it?"

Petey looked over at Raffy, who grunted and shrugged in response.

Then, before Petey could reply, Raffy said, "It's like this, man. You have the thing, you know…it's not set to, like, keep the thing going, man." He put up his hands in frustration. "There are a lot of complicated, you know, like, aspects, man. You can't just—"

"What he's trying to say," Petey interrupted, "is that you should have hooked up a Kerplexing Rectification Module. On top of that, you've got this thing screwed in so tight you'd think it was one of your freaky sex slaves or something."

She frowned at him. "The what?"

Petey stood up and pointed at the screw on the side of the rotation chamber. "That thing."

"It's called a screw."

"Yeah, thanks." The fallen angel pushed on. "You've got the damned thing so tight that it's causing unnecessary friction." He rubbed his chin. "We know *why* you did it, of course."

"Because it'll fall apart if it's too loose?" she said.

"Exactly." He nodded toward Raffy. "He came up with a floating chamber idea that solves the problem, especially if you tap into a bit of magic to give it a little extra pep." He used the tiny screwdriver in his hand to point at the mid-section. "I adjusted the chamber component like

Raffy said, and then I was loosening the screw here to set it just right."

A floating chamber? That was a brilliant idea, actually. She wasn't a fan of the idea to use magic, though. Then again, she could see how doing so could improve the efficiency of the weapon. Magic had a way of doing that, but it was a cheat in her estimation.

Madison may have been a lot of things, including a hacker, but a cheat? No. That was one thing she was not.

Still, the Stinkfoot's idea held merit.

"Why not just call it a floating chamber instead of a Krapmatic Rectal Mount?"

"It's the Kerplexing Rectification Module, man," Raffy said in a moment of clarity. "Names matter, man."

"He's right," Petey replied and then must have noticed her confused frown. He grunted and sighed. "You should really read a sci-fi series called *Platoon F*, specifically the parts about an engineer by the name of Geezer. If you do, you'll soon learn that naming things is key to the success of any product."

"Platoon F?"

Petey had swiped the weapon back from her hands and continued his tinkering for a few moments. He worked fast, but cleanly.

Madison was struck with instant fascination. Could it be that these two morons weren't morons at all? Was it possible the Stinkfoot was some kind of savant under all that weed-infused hair? Fallen angels—demons mixed with pixies—were known to be clever, cunning, and capable, but there wasn't a lot of information floating around regarding the infamous Stinkfoot.

She couldn't argue against Raffy's idea, however. It was solid. And while he may have been the brains, there was no way his massive hands could've handled the work Petey was rolling through like a seasoned expert.

"There," Petey said, holding up the gun, "give that a shot."

Madison wasn't sure if that was intended to be a pun or not, but since he wasn't smiling she assumed it wasn't.

She gave them both a look and then walked over to the small shooting booth, a contraption she'd created to allow her to test various weapons without having to go down to the main firing range.

The brrrrrrpt sound no longer had that high-pitched scraping she'd been struggling to resolve. It was smooth and silky, barely even vibrating as the miniature projectiles zipped out like a rushing river. Even better, there was zero kick.

Nice.

"Okay," she said, looking back at the dynamic duo, "you're either unbelievably lucky or incredibly smart."

Petey pointed at Raffy. "*He's* incredibly smart."

Raffy smiled, revealing his large teeth. "Like, you know, thanks, man."

"I'm more on the lucky side, but I'm good with my hands." The way he was wiggling his eyebrows at her made it crystal clear his statement had been intended to be somewhat dirty. "Let me know if you have any interest in that, *Mistress* Kane."

"That's like something I'd watch, man."

Ugh.

Madison immediately opened a channel to the entire

crew and said, *"From this point forward, everyone is to simply refer to me by my first name, Madison. Except for Rusty, he shall continue calling me by my full title."*

"Sweet," Rusty replied, which he quickly followed up with, "Sorry, Mistress."

Madison grimaced for a moment. *"And before you bother to ask why, I'll just say when a fallen angel makes a pass at you, calls you 'Mistress,' and he's got a dirty little smirk on his face,* and *then his Stinkfoot of a pal makes it clear he'd enjoy watching...well, it makes you rethink a lot of shit!"*

CHAPTER 6

Jin

The Cleaners appeared to be the model of efficiency, systematically gathering back every single person who had fled the park only minutes before. Using some form of technology that Jin couldn't understand if he tried, every normal soon found themselves leaving the park again, only this time with a renewed look of calm. It was rather impressive, something Jin wished he would have had access to during his assassination missions. To have everyone involved in the event suddenly forget it'd ever happened would have saved a lot of lives in the long run.

The normals had been gathered to a location that shielded them from the work other members of The Cleaners were doing, and for good reason.

Crews were using some kind of vacuum to suck up blood, chunks of flesh, and even complete body parts.

What couldn't fit through the nozzle ended up getting flashed by some kind of flamethrower. That's what it'd looked like, at any rate.

"This is kind of disturbing," he said, "and that's coming from me."

Raina giggled. "Yeah, the first time seeing something like this is a bit jarring, but you have to admit it's a damn good thing we've got people like this to do these jobs."

"I guess."

"Just don't get too close, chief," Rudy noted, standing next to Jin with his arms crossed as he admired the show. "Did that once and lost more than a few tail feathers."

"Chickens are drawn to light," Clive explained. "Werechickens are, anyway."

Rudy frowned at him and then glanced back at Jin. "It's wererooster, colon tooth. Quit trying to wind me up." Clive was grinning, proving Rudy's assessment had been correct. "Anyway, chief, there are a lot of things you'll see in this line of work that will bend your brain a bit. For instance, you've probably never witnessed a regular-looking dude roll out a big 'ol tail and whip it around."

Clive lost his grin. "Keep yapping, chicken dinner."

"Whatever you say, glue boy."

Glue boy? Ah, right. Horses, collagen, glue. Man, these guys were like a couple of brothers who were always seeking to one-up each other.

"Do these two ever stop?" he asked Raina via a direct connection.

"Not really, but it's mostly harmless. Now and then they'll beat the crap out of each other. The next day they're the best of pals again. It's kind of weird, but it seems to work for them."

Jin was going to press for more information until he noticed one of The Cleaners walking their way. Lacey was floating above him, talking him up like there was no tomorrow. It was strange since he was wearing a full protective suit that included a helmet with a one-way mirror face shield.

"And I was just after thinkin' maybe we had a few things in common," she said as the person stopped and looked up at her.

"Sorry, no."

Lacey shrugged. "Figured ye'd say that, but it was well worth a try."

"Dare I ask?" Jin asked.

"Lacey is always on the lookout for 'interesting' activities." It was odd, especially since Raina hadn't used her hands at all, but Jin definitely envisioned mental air quotes. *"I don't know a lot about leprechauns, so I can't really speak to the particulars. What I've learned has come from Chimi and she's never been all that interested in speaking about the things she and Lacey discuss when they're away from work unless it has to do with astrology or her strange deck of cards, of course."*

Jin wasn't about to dive into that discussion. He wouldn't have had the chance anyway, seeing as The Cleaner had stepped up to him and Raina.

"Where is Chief Fysh?"

"She's a Director now," Raina answered. Then she gestured toward Jin. "This is Chief Kannon. He's new, so go easy on him."

The Cleaner refocused on Jin, scanning up and down as if to size him up.

"Jin Kannon, assassin, one thousand confirmed kills."

It was said robotically. "Orphaned at a young age. Holds a romantic notion of the Old West, specifically the outlaw gunmen from the lore in the Badlands. Enjoys long walks on the beach, smooth jazz, and reading about history."

Jin was taken aback by the accuracy, but he wasn't loving how all his secrets were being thrown about like it was nothing.

"Yeah, great! You know me. Let's move on, okay?"

The rest of his crew tried to hold their mirth. They mostly failed.

The Cleaner pulled out a tablet, appearing oblivious to Jin's response. "New regulations require the head of any PPD party on-site sign the Post-Authorization & Acceptance form." He pointed at the tablet. "You'll want to read this carefully before signing."

After looking around at the rest of his crew, Jin took the tablet and began to read.

The signing party, who has signed below and has been witnessed as signing below by all parties who may or may not be within the radius of the signing party, and who therefore may or may not have actually witnessed said signing, agrees that all aspects of the cleaning process handled by The Cleaners on behalf of the Paranormal Police Department, specifically the San Diego precinct, has been done flawlessly and without fault, mishaps, derangement, or anything coming close to or even being considered potentially faultish. The signing party agrees they have personally inspected every square centimeter within a three-mile radius to ensure no residual supernatural remnants remain, are unaccounted for, and/or exist in any way, shape, or form relative to reality in this, or any other, dimension. Additionally, the signing party has agreed they have personally interviewed every normal who has been in the area, in the vicinity of the area, or has even considered traveling to the area at some point in the future— though not further out than sixty days—to verify they have no recollection or any pre-or-post-conceived notions of the event warranting the use of The Cleaners.

He looked up incredulously. "Are you being serious?"

The guy put his finger on the datapad and caused the screen to scroll up.

Please note that we are being completely serious.

Jin shook his head in disbelief. "And what, pray tell, happens should someone find anything in a square centimeter—which is ridiculous to expect a person to scour, by the way?"

He reached out again and scrolled further.

Should any remnants, blotches, blood stains, body parts, hairs, or any other potentially identifiable aspects of supernatural presence be left unaccounted for, or should any normal and/or persons claim awareness of knowledge, pre or post, regarding the event, the signing party agrees to be held personally responsible, which shall include a fine of no less than ten thousand dollars and no more than one million dollars. Additionally, the signing party understands that prison time will range between thirty days and thirty years, depending on the level of fault found, in addition to the damage done.

"This is fucking crazy," Jin said with a scoff. "I mean, come on, you've got to be kidding!"

Another scroll.

Please note that we are not kidding.

"Well, I'm not signing this."

Yet another scroll.

The lead officer who is in charge of the PPD officers on the field during a cleaning process is required by law to act as the signing party. Refusal to do so will result in immediate expulsion from the force, a one hundred thousand dollar fine, and two years of imprisonment.

He shot a look over at Raina. "Did you know about this?"

"Everyone does, chief. Comes with the job. Well, as of about three months ago, anyway." She gave him an apologetic look. "It's kind of new. The Cleaners used to avoid speaking to us at all, but officers kept pestering them."

"And so they got even by creating new laws."

"Yep."

Chimi pulled out a satchel and set it on the ground. She took out a small piece of blue cloth and unraveled it. There were three bones. She picked them up and rolled them, causing them to land slightly on each other.

"Hmmm," she said, turning her head to look up at Jin. "According to this, they've missed a lot of stuff, chief."

Shit.

"That means it's safe for you to sign," Rudy pointed out.

What?

"But I just told him it wasn't," Chimi argued.

"Which means it is," Rudy countered.

Everyone nodded in agreement, including The Cleaners guy.

Raina, being one of the more tactful members of the squad, used her direct connection. *"Remember how I explained that whatever Chimi comes up with is almost always inaccurate? Whatever she 'reads' in her cards or chakras or bones is never right. I should say it's* rarely *right. We rely on doing the opposite of her readings and things typically work out great."* She paused and added. *"She was correct about you, though, so it's not like she's* always *wrong."*

According to the document in front of him, it wasn't as if he had much of a choice in the matter regardless of how accurate Chimi's readings were. He either signed it or he was going to be facing jail time, not to mention losing a big chunk of change. At this point, being kicked off the PPD would've been fine with him, though. *That* part of the document was the only silver lining in the damn text.

With a grunt, he used his finger to sign on the line, all the while thinking it might have been worth losing the money and facing a couple of years in prison, too.

If nothing else, it was definitely one more item to put on the cons side of his mental pros/cons list.

He signed and handed the datapad back, hoping The Cleaners hadn't missed anything.

"All right," he said, a newfound level of angst hitting

his mind, "let's get our asses back to the office and figure out what the hell we're going to do next."

CHAPTER 7

Vestin

*V*estin was speaking with Emiliano. Technically, he was admonishing the man, and with good reason.

"Every time you go out you come back with the same number of people," he grumbled. "If you take ten soldiers with you, five of them are permanently killed and you capture five others we zombify in order to replace the five who died."

"Yes, My Lord?"

Vestin pinched the bridge of his nose.

"Well, that's not how it should be, Emiliano. The purpose of these raids is for you to *increase* our numbers, not lower them or keep them even. If that was all we were attempting to do, it would be better off for you to just stay here until we start fighting larger battles."

Emiliano shifted a few times in his stance. It was clear the zombie wasn't fully in league with Vestin on their topic of discussion, but he was holding back. In some respects, that's precisely what Vestin wanted his subordinates to do. From his point of view, followers should keep their ears open and their mouths shut.

But if his years in vampiric schools had taught him anything regarding failed leaders, it was that they utterly refused to listen to the points of view their inferiors held.

It pained Vestin to no end, but the last thing he wanted was to end up in one of those "Failed Leaders" tomes.

"You have something to say, Emiliano?"

After a bit of mental effort, which was only apparent because he kept stripping thin pieces of flesh off his body, Emiliano said, "It's just that we're fighters, My Lord. Our first thought isn't about personal safety or the safety of our crew."

"Shouldn't it be?"

"Before I was a zombie, I would say...mostly." He tore a few large strips of skin away. "In my current state, I quickly find myself driven by a level of power I've never known. It's intoxicating to throw people around, punch holes in their chests, and slice them in half with my new claws."

"Hmmm."

The thing was that Vestin could thoroughly understand where Emiliano was coming from. Wasn't he also infatuated with the power he held on his current throne? He had the right, of course, since he was the leader.

Still, power was power.

"I *do* see your point, Emiliano," Vestin said carefully, "and I must admit I hold a certain level of empathy for it, but we all must learn restraint regarding our personal desires in support of the greater goal." He pursed his lips and regarded the man. "You *do* understand that, yes?"

"Yes, My Lord."

"Excellent. Going forward, I expect you to work with your soldiers to ensure they understand it as well. Our purpose is to *build* the army. Please do keep that in mind."

"Yes, My Lord."

With that out of the way, even though Vestin felt certain things would continue as they had for some time yet; he turned his attention to Prender.

His second-in-command was fidgeting even more than Emiliano had been, only he wasn't tearing strips away from his person. His nails *did* have that "chewed-on" look, however. Prender seemed to mostly have his wits about him, but Vestin had noted more and more that the man held onto a lot of anxiety.

"Where are we with progress on *Shaded Past #13*?"

Prender whipped out his datapad, looking relieved.

"Actually, My Lord, we both received an email from Janet Smith today on that very topic." He ran his finger over the screen. "It says here that everything is ready, including the small building that will house recruits. In order to push forward you need only pay their initial invoice."

The sting of the words "pay their initial invoice" caused Vestin to shift in his chair. Did these people truly not understand that at some point they would *all* be servants in his realm? Seemingly not.

He recalled the contract he'd signed. It forbade him to take any action against the company or any of its employees or relatives, but laws were controlled by victors and Vestin was certain to be the victor in the war on San Diego. Soon after, his reach would extend to the corners of the world, and then he would set his sights on the Netherworld. Once that happened, *all* laws would be of his making. The contract with *Turner, Turner, and Smith* would instantly become moot, at which point Vestin would turn the screws heavily on everyone there, especially Janet Smith. Call him names, would she? Hah! Vestin would soon see about that.

For now, however, he would need to continue playing the game.

He took out his datapad and looked through his emails, not seeing the one from Janet Smith. That was curious. Why would she message Prender and not him? And didn't Prender say the email was sent to them both?

"I do not see the message in my inbox."

"That's odd, My Lord," Prender replied, tapping on his screen a few more times. "Ah, I see why. It appears she has used an incorrect email address for you."

"Oh?"

"Um, yes, My Lord."

Vestin grimaced, his eyes going dull. "What did she put?"

Prender tugged at his collar for a moment. "She used *thatfangedfart@vampyturdhaven.com*, My Lord."

"What? That's not even remotely close to my actual email address!" He pounded the arm of his throne, careful not to hit it too hard. He didn't want to cause it any permanent damage. Shaking his head, Vestin added, "At least it's not an email address anyone would have! That would be disastrous."

At just that moment, down in the depths of a building in the Badlands, a chime sounded on a datapad.

A lonely hand of an ancient vampire by the name of Lord Zantril, who had given up his pursuit of power many years prior, reached out to see who had contacted him, for he had not been contacted in a very long time.

"Janet Smith?" Zantril mused. "I don't recall anyone of that name. And she wants money?"

He glanced at the email address to make sure he was on the correct account. Sure enough, it read "thatfangedfart@vampyturdhaven.com."

"Must be some kind of spam," he grunted, before blocking the email address and deleting the message. "Blasted kids these days."

Vestin continued forcing himself calm.

"It concerns me that we must pay *before* seeing results," he pointed out. "Do I foot the bill on a meal before eating it?"

"At fast food places, you do," Emiliano said.

Vestin gave him a disgusted look. "I *do not* eat at fast food places." That wasn't completely true. He would, from time to time, sneak away and get himself a hot fudge sundae from that McDonald's establishment. Sometimes he'd even include a small order of their french fries for dipping. He wasn't about to admit to that, of course. "I speak of reputable restaurants." His words were nearly covered by the grumbling of his stomach, which always happened when he thought of those hot fudge sundaes.

Again, he shifted in his chair.

"I will get with Janet Smith and sort everything out," he stated. "Until then, let's work to *build* our army, gentlemen. Are we clear?"

They nodded in unison. "Yes, My Lord."

CHAPTER 8

Jin

They'd gotten back to the precinct and were absolutely beside themselves with what had happened. It'd been their second run-in with the zombies and the results hadn't been much better than the first time. From Jin's perspective, it had actually been much worse, and not just because he'd effectively signed a document that could quite literally destroy him should anyone find anything identifying about supers due to the attack.

That wasn't his biggest worry at the moment, however.

The fact was there was no way the San Diego PPD was going to be able to keep up with the zombies. They were too strong. On top of that, everyone knows zombies have a way of growing their numbers. Since Emiliano had spoken at their first meeting, and he'd seemed pretty damned intelligent when doing so, Jin had to believe it'd

JOHN P. LOGSDON & JENN MITCHELL

only be a matter of time before there were far more zombies than his crew could handle.

Hell, they could barely contain the number they'd faced so far.

"'We're going to need a bigger boat,'" said Clive.

Jin furrowed his brow at the man. "Boat?"

"Sorry, chief, it's a line from a movie called *Jaws*. It's about a shark that eats people and they try to chase it down in a boat that's not really big enough..." He looked around clearly recognizing that everyone was giving him a dull look. "Sorry."

"Well, you're not wrong," Jin said, bringing all their eyes back to him. "The fact is we're not going to be able to contain these zombies for long." He gave a quick nod to Clive. "Speaking of movies, we've all seen what happens when zombies gain a head of steam."

"We can handle it, chief," Raina declared, her positivity shining like a beacon.

Jin didn't want to burst her bubble, but wishful thinking tended to get people killed, at least in his old line of business.

"I'd love to agree with you, Raina, but the fact is all of you would be dead right now if I hadn't gotten my integration mostly reversed."

"Mostly?" said Rudy, his eyebrows up. "You mean you're not as deadly as you were? I mean damn, chief, your shooting was a thing to behold."

"Um...thanks." He would forever feel odd about receiving praise for that. "Anyway, if one of those things had tackled me before I'd had the chance to take out the others, we'd all be having this meeting in the Vortex.

Either that or we would've ended up serving in the zombie army ourselves."

Nobody challenged that assertion.

"We need more officers."

Lacey laughed.

Jin frowned at her. "Did I say something funny?"

Before either of them could reply, Raina spoke up. "Getting new officers in the PPD is pretty difficult, chief. It took Director Fysh months before she was allowed to requisition a new chief, and that was *after* they'd promised her a promotion. The paperwork alone is daunting."

He knew all about paperwork. Hell, even the document trail necessary to kick off an assassination in the Badlands took weeks to process, often forcing the assassin to go through multiple channels for approvals and legal protections. Gone were the days of, "See that guy? I don't like that guy. Kill that guy." BAM! "Thanks. Here's a couple hundred bucks." It was all CYA—Cover Your Ass—documentation protocols now, which was admittedly better than spending months on trial and years in prison, but that didn't make it fun.

This was different, though. If the zombie issue went unchecked, they were going to overrun San Diego.

"These are obviously not normal circumstances," Jin pointed out. "The powers that be will have to see that, right?"

More laughter.

Again, Raina was the one to reply. "There are always things like this, chief." She bounced her head around. "Okay, not *always*. We have weeks or months where stuff is kind of quiet, but inevitably a group of jerks raise their heads and start causing big trouble. I'll admit this one is one of the worst I've seen. Sometimes it's pretty easy, of course, but there are times when it requires thinking outside of the box." She gave him a weary look. It looked strange on her otherwise cheery face. "Backup isn't really a thing."

Originally, Jin had been led to believe things went relatively smoothly in the PPD, at least as far as the San Diego precinct went. That said, he could've argued that being an assassin wasn't all that challenging, but he'd had one thousand confirmed kills. In other words, when he started out in that line of work it'd been hellish as he learned to navigate his way through. A few years in it was just another day on the job.

Still, Raina had noted this kind of thing wasn't exactly abnormal so Jin seriously had to ask himself if he wanted to deal with that all the time. Wasn't he trying to escape this kind of drama?

It was yet another negative to add to his list.

He turned his attention to Hector. "I don't suppose your—"

Hector held up a hand. "Don't bother, Chief Kannon. I've already considered it and there's no way I can get reinforcements. My boss wouldn't dare risk sending more people into this area, and I think it should be pretty clear why."

It was.

"I have an idea."

Jin turned toward the voice. "Yes, Miss Ka...um, Madison?"

"While we're not going to get the numbers, we *could*

bring someone to the table who can't be turned, would be quite fast, have nearly unlimited stamina, would be able to fire with near-perfect accuracy, and would also have the strength of multiple supers."

Everyone's faces went slack, making it apparent they all knew what she was talking about. Too bad Jin was on the outs. Eventually—should he ultimately choose to stay —he'd catch the various nuances and insider information everyone else caught readily, but that wasn't today.

"And how would we do that?" he asked.

"Rusty."

"Yes, Mistress?"

"I wasn't calling you. Be silent." There was no response as she refocused on Jin. "A number of PPD precincts have built out an android body for their station's AI. Some have turned out well."

"Some?"

"There is no set methodology yet, Chief Kannon," she replied pedantically. "That said, there are a number of papers and processes written that have led to advances and best practices, each demonstrating growth and practicality in the science."

The problem Jin had was it was all about technology, and that just wasn't a strength of his. But did it need to be? No. He simply had to have faith that Madison was capable enough to make sure there wouldn't be any major issues.

Was Jin that confident in her ability?

The PPD recognized her capabilities or she wouldn't be in this position, so clearly she was solid at what she did.

JOHN P. LOGSDON & JENN MITCHELL

Why was he even thinking that way? Was it because he spent so many years working solo? Probably. Jin wasn't one who trusted people easily. He *wanted* to. Hell, probably even *longed* to. But he didn't. Trust and respect took time. To be fair, everyone on his crew probably felt the same about him, and they were right to do so.

Regardless, was there really any other choice at this point? If Madison could create an android that was faster than all of them, stronger than all of them, and—most importantly—could *not* be turned into a zombie, Jin would be nuts to turn down the option.

"What do you need from me in order to get it done?"

"You have to get Director Fysh to approve it."

"Okay," he said, squaring his shoulders, "no problem."

Everyone laughed again.

Jin sighed and noticed something was off. "Where's Chimi?"

All fingers pointed toward the conference room. It was dimly lit and Jin was certain he could see wafts of smoke floating up. Squinting, he saw Chimi through the light fog. Unless his eyes were fooling him, she was dressed somewhat like the fortune tellers he'd seen in a few topside historical books.

"What's she doing?"

"Her crazy *ass*-trology stuff," Lacey said with a hint of venom.

The way she'd said it made clear the leprechaun didn't share in her partner's beliefs. Jin didn't either, but he was more of a science-minded kind of guy. That's not to be confused with a tech mind. Again, no. He merely preferred evidence over faith.

He had learned to temper himself over the years when it came to being tolerant of how others perceived the world, though. It often colored his view of people when he saw how easily they were duped by certain things, but he'd slowly learned that everyone had their own path in life. The experiences of each person were valid in one way or another, even if the realities were suspect. It was *their* reality. As long as they weren't hurting anyone, and as long as they weren't trying to convince him of something he knew held no evidence of fact, he did his best to avoid offering his unsolicited two cents.

It wasn't easy.

"And why is she doing this?"

"She always does, chief," Raina explained. "It's her way of trying to see what we can do to succeed."

He nodded and gave Raina a sideways glance. "But you said she's always wrong?"

"Very nearly, yes."

"Which," Madison chimed in, "could be argued means she's nearly always right, just in the wrong direction."

Exactly, and that was weird. Scientific? No. But definitely weird.

"Well," he said with a shrug, "it's not like we have much else to go on at this point, aside from hoping we can convince Director Fysh to allow us to build out Rusty." The laughter was more subdued that time. "I guess let's go and see what Chimi has to say."

The laughter stopped, having been replaced with groans.

CHAPTER 9

Emiliano

render had come into Emiliano's section of the small lair and he appeared to be fidgeting. The zombie wasn't sure if it was because the space felt so confined or if something else was going on. Emiliano hadn't exactly been great with reading people *before* he'd been turned into a member of the undead. Now, he was terrible at it, or it was possible that he cared even less than he had before.

Yeah, it was probably that.

"Do you require something?" Emiliano asked, showing only the slightest bit of respect.

Prender may have been Vestin's second-in-command, which would technically mean Emiliano was third in line, as far as he knew, but Prender had no direct hold over him. Vestin had "discussed" Prender being in charge of Emiliano, only there'd been a hesitance in his voice. That was how Emiliano had chosen to remember it, anyway. If

Vestin wasn't certain that Prender was cut from the right cloth, Emiliano wouldn't be either.

The man was rubbing his hand against one of the walls as if studying it.

"It's far too cramped in this lair for the army we'll be building, don't you think?"

"I do." And it was, but Emiliano knew that wasn't the reason Prender was standing here. "You're not telling me something."

Prender let out a large sigh and threw up his hands. "Look, I hate to do this but Lord Vestin told me I had to, so here goes."

Emiliano tilted his head. "Go on."

"You have to perform better," Prender said, looking as if he was trying to be forceful. He was failing at it. If anything, it'd come out more like a whine or possibly a plead. "I don't like getting in trouble and I'm sure you don't either."

"I'm fine with it, as long as it's warranted."

"Exactly, and…what?"

Honestly, *this* was the man who was to take over should anything happen to Lord Vestin. Second-in-command meant a person would graduate to the top spot should the need arise. But how could Vestin be so foolish as to think Prender was capable of handling such responsibility?

Was Vestin a bigger fool than Emiliano thought?

He felt an immediate tightening in his guts and a level of dread and guilt in his thoughts that threatened to make him want to cut his own head off.

It had to have been caused by the venom of his Lord.

There was no other sensible explanation. He'd thought of something about Vestin that made clear in his own mind he would personally take over the army should his Lord prove unworthy and…

"Shit," he gasped, falling forward while gripping his stomach in anguish.

"Oh, no," Prender said, rushing to Emiliano's side. "I didn't mean to make you ill, Emiliano! We just need to do better, that's all. It's nothing to make yourself sick over, man!"

It was all Emiliano could do not to vomit. That he'd managed to keep the arm he'd feasted on an hour before attacking the park was amazing.

Too bad his ass hadn't gotten the memo.

A fountain of shit sprung from his bottom like Old Faithful. It hit the walls, it struck other zombies, and it cannoned into Prender—square in the face.

"Oh my god!" Prender rasped, vomiting all over the place moments later.

Everyone in the room began to laugh, including Emiliano, which resulted in his ass launching even more ejecta that further resulted in Prender's puke-fest gaining momentum.

Prender rushed from the room as Emiliano fought to get back to his feet.

"We'll try to do better," Emiliano called out after the man while the zombies continued laughing. Then, under his breath, Emiliano added, "You stupid shithead."

He smiled at his own pun.

CHAPTER 10

Jin

The crew pushed into the conference room. Chimi had set everything up just so, including a small fog machine that was obviously the cause of the eerie mist. She was wearing brightly-colored clothing, all wrapped around her in some fashion or another. It definitely had that gypsy vibe, which looked strange on Chimi, especially the head wrap part because it was placed in such a way as to surround her single eye.

Behind her hung a little wooden sign that was being held up by a single thumbtack.

Chimi the Fortune Teller
Palm Reading: $50
Tarot Card Reading: $100
Crystal Ball Scrying: $150
The works: $250 (save $25!)

Okay, so math clearly wasn't her strong suit.

Chimi looked up at Jin and then glanced at the chair across from her. He fused his eyebrows together, peering over at Raina for guidance.

Raina opened a connection with him. *"You're the chief, chief."*

"Okay?"

"Something this big requires you to be the one she does her, um, readings for."

The list of cons for sticking with this job was growing. Wasn't it bad enough they were dealing with a zombie infestation? Wasn't it bad enough they were having to work with the local crime cartel when they should have been imprisoning them instead? Wasn't it bad enough that he'd *still* not been able to sit quietly at the beach and watch a single fucking sunset?

He closed his eyes for a moment and drew in a slow breath through his nose, steadying himself. He'd done this many times over his years as an assassin. It was the only thing that centered him whenever things ran amok.

Feeling somewhat better, he sat down and put his hands on the table.

"Oh, hello," Chimi said. She then quickly glanced down to her right and murmured to herself for a moment before looking back at him. "I am say-your-name-here, a world-renowned fortune teller." She pointed up at the sign behind her. "What is your name?"

Jin grimaced but kept it together. "Jin Kannon."

"And what brings you into my shop today, Jin Kannon?"

She pushed over a hand-written cue card.

He looked at it and shook his head, before reading the words. "I'm here seeking knowledge, oh wise..." He stopped and brought his eyes up. "Seriously?"

Chimi tapped on the card.

Another deep breath. "I'm here seeking knowledge, oh wise and miraculous one."

She pulled the card back and turned her attention again to whatever it was beside her.

Having been an assassin for many years, Jin had learned a few tricks. One of them was to use a small mirror so he could quickly see what was around a corner without the need to stick his neck out and potentially have his head blown off. Flicking his wrist, a small mirror extended from a stick and he peered down at it.

After a few quick angle adjustments, he was able to see that Chimi was referring to a book. The text was backwards, but after a few seconds, he'd figured it out.

Fortune Telling for Dummies

Jin couldn't hold back from rolling his eyes as he retracted the mirror.

By then, Chimi's focus had returned and she pushed over a box.

"I'm guessing you want the works," she stated. "I take Visa, Mastercard, Discover, and American Express—but only if you pay the up-charge—and, of course, cash." She leaned forward slightly. "I used to take PayPal, too, but they were a pain to work with."

"*She's joking, right?*" Jin asked Raina.

"*She's not, chief.*"

At this point, Jin was taking more deep breaths than regular ones.

He pulled out his wallet and realized that he didn't have any way to pay for stuff topside. Credit card companies weren't the same in the Netherworld as they were up here, and the currency was vastly different. That said, there *were* places that handled currency exchanges, so he grabbed the largest bill he had from his wallet and set it in front of her.

"I don't have topside currency, but I believe exchanging this will provide double what you're asking for."

Her single eye opened wider than usual and she reached out and grabbed the bill. She studied it for a second, which included a sniff test, rubbing her fingers across it, and giving it a lick.

"Seems legit," she said before stuffing it down her shirt. "Okay, um…" Chimi went back to the book again for a moment. "Ah, yeah. You want your palm read?"

No, he did not, but he was quickly recognizing what he wanted in this situation didn't matter. He was doing this for his team, for Chimi. It was idiocy in his mind, and it was an utter waste of time—time they did *not* have.

So, reluctantly, he said, "Sure," and put his hand out, understanding that would be the next step in hopefully bringing a quick end to this charade.

In a flash, Chimi grabbed a small red container, dipped a brush in it, and then ran that across Jin's hand.

He used his other hand to facepalm.

"You're kidding me," he said. "You literally just painted my palm red."

Without responding, she grabbed his hand and started running her finger over it, smearing the red paint around. It tingled and then burned. He gritted his teeth at the pain but held strong.

"You will have a short life," she said in an ominous tone. "You will die before reaching the age of twenty-five."

"I'm thirty-seven, Chimi."

She turned her head slightly and twisted his hand. "Oh, sorry. Was reading it upside down."

Jin actually had to bite his lip that time in order to keep from saying something. He hadn't even bothered complaining to Raina. There was no point. It was clear that everyone was either enjoying the scene or that they felt there was some value in it.

If Madison was correct, all they had to do was flip everything Chimi said around and they might find some accuracy in her "readings."

The thought that he only had another fifteen years to live was a bit concerning, but considering how he'd nearly died hundreds of times as an assassin it was fifteen more years than he should've had. Actually, he should've died many years ago. If he really thought about it, twenty-five was probably more accurate than fifty-two, even though he'd managed to survive much longer than that.

He shrugged as Chimi handed him one of those wet napkin pouches.

"You can wipe your hand clean," she said. "There's nothing else on there worth noting, except to say you might consider moisturizing."

Jin wiped his hand clean, fighting to hold back a grunt.

For her next trick, Chimi pulled out some cards and

laid them on the table. This deck looked a fair bit different than the ones he'd seen in a book about mystics. It'd been a Badlands book, not one from Topside, though the Topside ones were likely based on the Badlands ones anyway. Regardless, he assumed the cards she used were specific to the Cyclops style of tarot.

Her methodology was different from what he'd seen before, too.

She shuffled the cards like a blackjack dealer at one of Infernal City's top casinos, even going as far as doing one-handed shuffling. Jin assumed she was showing off at first, but the look on her face was etched in pure concentration. She spread the cards out in a single line and then flipped the end card to make them all go from their backs to front. Next, she scooped them up and moved her hands apart, bending the deck until each card launched across and landed in her opposite hand.

It was impressive until she finished the show and fanned the cards out in front of Jin.

"Pick a card," she said. "Any card."

"Come on! Really?"

"Just do it, chief."

"Ridiculous."

He reached out to snag one from the deck.

"No, not that one," she said, taking it away from him and setting it on the table. "I don't know how to read that one, yet."

Jin squinted at her and then shook his head and grabbed a different card.

"Perfect!"

Chimi lowered the rest of the deck, setting it on the

table as she slowly spun the selected card around, lying it face up in front of him. It contained the image of a two-headed cyclops, each looking in the opposite direction of the other. Aside from that, they looked pretty much identical.

"Do you know what this card means?" she asked.

"Can't say I do."

"It's the Two-Looks card, Jin Kannon," Chimi explained as if that was intended to mean something.

"Ah," he said, playing along somewhat sarcastically, "the Two-Looks card. Should've been obvious, I suppose."

Chimi sat up straight and eyed him for a moment. "So you *do* know what it means?"

"Certainly. It means whatever you've been taught it means by someone who was taught by someone else what it means, going back as far in time as required until we find the original person who created that card and completely made up a definition for it so they could use it to make money and/or control people who were too dimwitted to realize it was all a sham." He grinned at her. "Am I close?"

If you've never seen a Cyclops raise an eyebrow, you haven't lived.

In response, Chimi leaned over and began studying her book again. She flipped the pages back and forth a number of times. She'd clearly landed on the page she was hunting because she began mumbling the words she'd read.

Finally, she glanced back up at him with a shocked look.

"You *do* know how this works!"

He did. The thing that surprised him was that a how-to book on the subject would note it.

At this point, he figured it was worth continuing with the process. He *had* paid a decent chunk of change, after all. Besides, if what the rest of the team said was true about her being wrong so often, it could be valuable to hear what she had to say. Yes, even a diehard skeptic such as Jin could see the wisdom in "nearly always wrong" meaning if you did the opposite of what she said, you may be in good shape.

"So what, pray tell, did the original person claim that card to mean?" he ventured, trying to appear interested.

Chimi *did* look excited, which made Jin feel like a bit of a heel for how he was acting. It might have been a silly piece of pseudoscience to him, but it was clearly important to Chimi. Plus, it wasn't like it was hurting anyone…possibly.

Hmmm.

"It means," she started, "that you will face someone of importance and you won't see eye-to-eye." Chimi looked up at him. "I'm guessing that means Director Fysh is going to decline your request."

"Yes!" said Madison with a fist pump. Jin frowned at her, to which she replied, "Sorry."

One didn't often see a succubus apologize.

"Right," Jin said, turning his attention back to Chimi. "Is that it then? Are we done now?"

"Not quite," she replied, dropping the card before pulling out a crystal ball and setting it between them. "I still have to look into your future." She wiped her huge nose. "You paid for it, so I should do it."

"Absolutely," he agreed, motioning for her to continue before putting his hands on the table.

Chimi moved her fingers all around the glass orb. She was chanting something Jin couldn't make out, but it sounded like she was saying, "peanut butter" over and over again.

He didn't ask.

Suddenly, she lowered her hands and leaned forward, gazing into the sphere with a mixture of hope and fascination.

"I see...I see...a...hand," she said. "It's distorted a little, but its fingers are moving, like they're tapping on a table or something."

Jin sighed yet again. She was merely seeing his actual hand through the orb. To test his theory, he crossed his first finger over his second.

"The fingers have crossed!"

He then spread them apart rapidly and began closing and reopening them over and over again.

"Now they're making a scissors kind of motion." She looked up at him excitedly. "I've never seen this happen before, chief...erm...Jin Kannon! It must be significant."

As she was looking at him, he carefully took his arm off the table.

When she refocused on the orb, a frown formed. She stood up and looked down at the object, then she glanced into it from various angles, until she sunk low enough for her face to light up yet again.

"Now, I see the entire team, though it's like I'm looking at them through water." She scratched her head again. "And I'm not with them for some reason."

"*Honestly?*" he said to Raina.

"Chimi," Raina said aloud, "remember that you have to quickly cover the crystal ball or you'll forget what your vision means?"

"Huh?" Chimi looked confused for a moment and then she quickly covered the ball with a dark towel. "Sorry, it sometimes captures me."

"Uh huh," said Jin, thinking they really needed to get back to work. "Give me the quick version of what it showed please?"

"It showed that I wasn't on the team anymore, chief," she replied, dismayed enough that she hadn't referred to him by his full name. "And since it showed your hand, and you were drumming your fingers, and then you made a 'cutting' motion, I'm guessing you're going to fire me at some point."

That put him in a bad spot, especially since a quick study of the room showed a number of disappointed frowns. They knew better than to believe this stuff, yet they were clearly miffed about it anyway! Unbelievable!

But what could he say? If he told her there was no way he was going to fire her, she would think he didn't believe in her ability to tell the future. He didn't, obviously, but how was he going to tell her that?

"Well, Chimi," he stated carefully as he stood back up, "I will tell you that I believe you're one of the best officers I've ever met." He hadn't met many. "You carry yourself with honor, you fight hard, and you have yet to do anything I would consider less than terrific. I sure can't imagine wanting to lose an officer like you, Chimi, so I can only hope there's a different reason for what you saw and that maybe, at some point, a better reason will reveal itself." He stopped at the door and turned back. "Right now, however, I have to hope that I can somehow convince Director Fysh to allow us to build that android."

"Cards say she won't," Chimi reminded him.

"Right."

CHAPTER 11

Jin

They were seated in a room that was accessed via a hidden door in Jin's office. Raina, being the ever-helpful one on the team, had shown him how to open it. The door itself would only respond to him, which he assumed the PPD had been configured during his first time walking in the building. In other words, it was probably part of the dataset that Guard Levi Snoodle had compiled when Jin originally arrived on site.

The room wasn't exactly spacious, and there was only one chair, but it was roomy enough for three people to stand around in.

"You have to sit in the chair, chief," Raina pointed out. "The connection won't happen unless you do."

Maybe it was his chivalrous nature, but he felt awkward taking a seat while the two ladies with him stood. Something told him not to say that aloud, though. He feared doing so would result in him getting a verbal lashing. That made him wonder if he would've felt the same about taking a seat if those with him had been Rusty and Clive. He didn't think he would.

Maybe it *was* time to rethink his stance on certain things.

For now, he took the seat and waited.

Thankfully, it wasn't long before a shaded image appeared in front of him. He knew it was Director Fysh, but he was suddenly having trouble remembering what she looked like. That was odd considering Jin had a pretty solid memory when it came to recalling faces. It was kind of important for an assassin to have that ability. Right now, however, it was as though she would fade in and out of his consciousness like he was trying to bring up the details of a dream he'd had upon waking. It was there, but...not.

"Chief Kannon?" she said. Her voice was familiar, at least. "If you're contacting me so soon, things must be worse off than I'd anticipated, and I anticipated they'd be pretty bad."

"They are, yes," he replied. "The zombie attack in the park was pretty rough." He lifted a finger and began to wag it. "By the way, I met with The Cleaners for the first time and it seems I had to sign my life away based on—"

"All part of the job, Chief Kannon," Director Fysh interrupted. "Can't be helped. Moving along, tell me about the zombie situation and what we're doing about it."

Jin stopped wagging his finger, feeling a bit defeated.

"Right." He sighed and lowered his hand. The accumulation of negatives on his pros/cons list was growing. "We were able to stop the attack, but we were admittedly fortunate to do so. In a nutshell…"

"We got lucky," finished Raina for him. She then winced and said, "Sorry, chief."

"She's right. We got lucky. If one thing had gone a different way, we'd not be having this call right now." Jin adjusted in his chair, considering removing his hat. He didn't. "We need more bodies, Director."

There was a moment of silence.

Jin anticipated that. In fact, he was counting on it. According to Madison, moving Rusty into the body of an android was going to be the most likely line of assistance the crew was going to get. So Jin was doing the old "Ask for a cake and you might get a cookie" line of negotiation.

"I know you're new to all of this, Chief Kannon," the Director said, "but adding more officers to your squad is far more of a challenge than you currently comprehend. They don't just grow on trees. It takes time, preparation, and paperwork. Simply locating qualified recruits is difficult enough." She grunted. "Honestly, it's damned hard. Counter to what you may believe, there aren't a ton of people who actually *want* to be officers in the PPD. It's a tough life and people know it."

A thought struck. "What about Snoodle and the rest of the guards? They all seem starstruck by us, and they made it clear to me when I first arrived that they were dying for a chance to become PPD officers."

This time the silence lasted even longer.

"How do I say this diplomatically?" she replied finally. "Okay, let's put it this way: The guards downstairs are excellent at being guards, that's why they're guards. But each of them has gone through the field test scenarios multiple times and has failed miserably. We can't risk that in real-life situations."

Jin decided to push a little harder. "I was never given a field test, Director Fysh, and I was allowed on as the chief."

"You *are* a field test, Chief Kannon. Honestly, you surpass the requirements by a fair margin."

And yet even he'd been seconds away from having his ass handed to him by the zombies. On top of that, Jin's officers *had* gotten their shit rocked. If Snoodle and his crew weren't even as solid as the normal cops, they would be minced meat right now. Actually, they'd be zombies, and that'd be even worse.

"Point taken," Jin acquiesced. "Okay, so we're not getting any additional bodies?"

"Sorry, no," Director Fysh responded, "but since Miss Kane is standing in there with you, I'm assuming you have something else in mind?"

Jin gave Madison a nod.

"First off," she said, "it's Madison now."

"Oh?"

"Long story. Anyway, I knew we weren't going to be getting additional officers. One look at the history of this place and you instantly understand just how hard that is." She shook her head, probably thinking how asinine it was, or that she was playing a part. Being a succubus gifted her with some pretty heavy manipulation techniques. "Anyway, I'm here to propose we shift Rusty into the body of an android."

The laugh that came from Director Fysh's side of the

room was immediate. It also wasn't the kind of laugh you heard when someone thought something was genuinely funny.

"Come on, Miss…Madison," she said. "You can't be serious. The budget for something like that is well beyond what I'm able to garner."

"Actually," Madison said in a smooth tone, "it really isn't."

"Oh?"

Crossing her arms and looking more than a bit apprehensive, Madison admitted something she clearly had not wanted to admit. "I've been building a body for Rusty for a couple of years now. Everything has been done on the sly with the excesses in funding my department has been provided. You see, I know how the system works. If you request a budget and you don't meet it, your budget next year will be docked automatically. However, if you meet or slightly exceed it, you'll either retain your budget or even get it marginally increased."

"Clever girl," said Director Fysh, though she didn't sound pleased. "You took the leftover amounts each year and funneled it into a secret project that not even the chief of the precinct knew about."

It wasn't a question.

"Would it have been allowed any other way?" Madison replied rhetorically.

Jin was assuming the worst since it was so quiet in the room at that moment you could have heard a moth fart. Madison had effectively embezzled from the department, though not for personal gain. It was a gray line. Depending on which side of that line Director Fysh chose to place it, Madison was either going to be a hero or she was going to be incarcerated.

Knowing Madion's history with the law, Jin knew she was taking an enormous risk in her admission.

"I should probably throw you in jail for that, Madison," the Director ultimately said, "but I have to admit that I'm mostly jealous I hadn't thought to do the same thing on numerous occasions."

Whew.

"But wait," Director Fysh added quickly, "you said you've already been working on it?"

"Completed it, actually," Madison stated. "I just have to have an official approval or it'll be obvious that I used PPD funds without prior knowledge."

"Ah. Well, I'll need to back-date a few documents then, won't I?"

Madison cracked a grin. "I've already gotten them written for you. They just need a signature."

"You are something, Madison, though I fear I should return myself to calling you Miss Kane after this little admission of yours." She laughed. "Okay, I would imagine having an android is going to help immensely. Have you considered anything else?"

Jin was about to respond when Madison said, "Well, I've got these little guns I've been working on lately. They're just like the gun Raina uses, though far smaller. Small enough to fit into a holster, in fact."

"Wow," said Raina. Jin agreed but kept his "Wow" to himself.

"If I could get about twenty-five thousand, or at least

get some equipment assigned here pronto, I could work with Raffy and Petey to build these out pretty quickly."

Raina and Jin gave her looks of astonishment.

"Raffy and Petey?" said Raina.

"Yeah," agreed Director Fysh, "what have they got to do with this?"

Madison was shaking her head in disbelief as she replied, "I wouldn't have believed it either, gang, but those two are basically savants when it comes to working with tech."

That time, everyone said, "Wow."

CHAPTER 12

Madison

It took wearing an industrial nasal-filtration system for Madison to manage working so closely with Raffy. She'd never realized how much a Stinkfoot...well, stank. The most interesting part had been how the smell truly *did* come from the creature's feet. It permeated straight up into Raffy's fur, settling there as if becoming one with the follicles.

She only knew this because she'd done some quick research on the species in order to help her tweak her nose plugs.

"So what's the plan, doll?" asked Petey, batting his eyelashes at her while lying on his stomach with his chin resting on his hands. It was clear he was smitten. "Shall I just watch as you move around the room in your perfect body?"

That kind of attention would normally turn her gears, but unless he vibrated she couldn't really see anything working out between them. Still, it was apparent Petey knew what it meant to play the game when it came to succubus relations. He was feeding her ego. She liked having her ego fed, of course. Too bad for him, she'd grown to the point where she was able to control her more animalistic urges.

Mostly, anyway.

But his attitude had to be nipped in the bud or it was going to be a problem.

So, she gave him a stern stare, crossed her arms, allowed her tone to grow dark, and said, "You will either do your job or you'll be punished, and that's as far as our relationship will ever go."

"Oooh, I like that," he said as his little body rocked back and forth slightly, "especially the part about me being punished."

Madison wasn't amused. "I'm serious, you tiny turd."

"Nice."

Her frustration grew. "Look, asshole, either you get professional really damned fast or I'm going to spank your miniature ass!"

"Petey like spanky," he cooed.

Madison snarled and brought her face close to his. "I swear to whatever god you believe in that if you don't shape up fast, worm, I'll whip you to within an inch of your life."

"Ahhhhg!" Petey yelped as his face turned red and his eyes began to bulge. His body contorted a few times and then relaxed, leaving him to lie still, grinning from ear to ear. "Thank you, Mistress." That was followed by a yawn, him curling up, and then falling fast asleep.

Madison stood there with her jaw hanging open. She should have known better, of course, but she was actually *trying* to be normal. Thinking back over her words, it was clear she'd been anything but normal.

"Man," said Raffy, who was busily studying the body of the android on the other table, "I don't, like, think that worked, like, you know, how you meant it to."

Madison was clearly going to need to change her tactics when it…um…"came" to Petey.

"Not easy to shake being a succubus, you know."

"Like, no, I don't, but yeah."

How could he? How could anyone but another succubus or incubus know what it was like? Actually, there was *one* other super who knew. He was an amalgamite, who was also the chief of the Las Vegas PPD. Ian Dex was his name. She sighed at the thought of him and then quickly cleared her throat and refocused on the task at hand.

They had to get Rusty's brain into the android. When it came to most things in life, Madison was pretty confident. This, however, was *not* most things. There was a real chance that Rusty would be lost if she made any mistakes. She was pretty sure she'd done everything to prepare the body for this moment, but there was always the risk that it'd fail. If that happened, bye-bye Rusty.

Honestly, it was one of the primary reasons she wanted Raffy and Petey to assist her.

If things went sideways, she needed someone to blame.

Bah!

No, that wasn't true. Actually, it *was* true, but she

refused to allow herself to think that way. Placing blame was something only weak-minded people did. Cowards. Quitters. Gutless fools. Succubi.

She seriously hated to admit that, but it was a fact. Her kind wasn't known for taking the blame for things, even if they were caught red-handed doing it. Narcissistic behavior was a way of life with them, even if not all succubi had the actual affliction. It was usually the incredibly-less-than-attractive ones who *did* have it, and they had it in droves. It also fell to the massively moronic ones of her kind. Match those two detractors in a single person, and you have a recipe for narcissism that couldn't be beaten.

That was a learned behavior for people like Madison, and she no longer wanted to be like that.

It just took effort.

"Have you had a chance to go over everything, Raffy?" she asked, though it pained her to do so.

"I, like, did dude." He held up the datapad she'd given him when they walked in. "Righteous reading. If I was, like, on shrooms, this would be wigging me out." He smiled, showing a set of pearly whites that stood as a complete contrast to the rest of him. "Truth, though, your dude's gonna combust if you, like, try to hookify him without, you know, really pumping up the specs, dig?"

Madison furrowed her brow. She did *not* dig.

"Pumping up the specs?"

A yawn sounded behind her. Petey was awake and stretching. That was fast. Madison knew he was part pixie and part demon, though, and refractory periods for both were wickedly short.

"He's saying that you haven't installed an Operating System yet," Petey replied. He got up and flittered over to the other table. "Don't ask me why he calls that 'pumping the specs,' cause I have no idea. But that's what he means."

Raffy appeared miffed. "It's because, like, you know, you're pumping the specs, man. I mean, there are a lot of complicated aspects, you know? If you can't follow the jello, then how can, like, the jello follow you?"

Petey shrugged at Madison. "No idea what the fuck that meant, but anyway, you have to install the OS before going any further."

Of course, she did! Ack! It was simply stupid of her not to think about it. But wait, why would that matter? Wouldn't it just fail to initiate the transfer, stating the android wasn't prepared?

She grabbed the datapad and started scrolling through the documentation.

"If you're, like, hunting for the deets, dude, it's on page 312."

Madison scoffed, thinking there was no way a Stinkfoot could possibly know...

Damn it. It *was* on page 312.

The base configuration assumes the person putting the android together has enough common sense to install an Operating System prior to attempting the transfer of the AI. Failure to do so would certainly result in loss of data and the likely destruction of the AI. Since this is beyond obvious, no integrity checking has been coded into the system.

That was dumb. People made mistakes all the time. Why in the world would they...

Note that if you try to come back at us with the tired "People make mistakes" argument, just know that if you make screwups that bad when building out something as complex as an android, you're far too dumb to be building out androids.

Madison sighed and then connected the cable to her main laptop. Once it was in place and registered as stable, she initiated the installation of the Operating System. If the OS failed, that *would not* be her fault. It was part of the delivery package and she'd been sure to verify the latest updates and patches had been part of the build.

"What's that?" asked Petey, pointing at the massive lump in the android's pants.

Recalling what these two had told her about naming things, she said, "That's the, um, ExtendoPackage 1000." She found herself rather liking that name. "It's my invention. It allows me to choose the size of his—"

Surprisingly, Petey waved his hands to stop her from talking. "No, no! That's okay! I don't want to know any more about it!"

"Does that bother you, *little* man?" She couldn't resist.

Petey gave her an irritated look and then said, "Let's just finish the job. There are zombies out there to kill, in case you've forgotten?"

Madison smirked, recognizing he *did* have an issue with being...smaller.

"Touchy, touchy."

CHAPTER 13

Jin

J in was getting a bit antsy. He knew Madison, Raffy, and Petey were all working on Rusty, but all he could think about was how each minute they weren't in the field was another minute the zombies could be wiping people out. His concern mostly came from the integration crap he'd endured, obviously, but he knew there was more to it than merely that. He'd always had a thing about protecting the innocent. It was the key reason he'd refused more contracts over his years than he'd taken. While he never technically "protected the innocent" in those instances, since they were undoubtedly killed by another assassin at some point or another, he felt he'd done his part by not pulling the trigger himself. It was admittedly a weak argument, but it was all he had.

As the chief of the San Deigo PPD, he was actually able to genuinely protect people, and while he'd only just started on the job, he rather liked how that felt.

Was it possible that was a positive for his pros/cons list?

It clearly was, but there were so few pros on the list at the moment that it wouldn't be enough to hold much water. Then again, shouldn't each point carry weight? It's not just the number of items filling each column, but how much each of them means, right? Isn't that how it's supposed to work?

He quickly thought back over the list and immediately recognized that "Protecting people" was easily canceled out by "Selling soul to The Cleaners."

Yeah, his list was definitely *not* in favor of sticking around once the zombie invasion was dealt with, assuming it ever got resolved. If it didn't, Jin would either be dead or he'd end up as a zombie himself. In either case, he would no longer care about his position as the chief, and his pros/cons list would become moot.

Just as he was about to check if Raina had any insights regarding how long stuff like this took, Madison walked around the corner with Raffy and Petey in tow.

He jumped to his feet and rushed out the office door.

"What happened?" he asked, noting there was no Rusty to be seen. "Did it fail?"

Madison smiled and snapped her fingers. "Worm, come here."

Two seconds later an incredibly attractive man walked around the corner. He stood about Jin's height, had perfectly-combed blonde hair, was lanky, though muscular, carried a flawless jawline, and wore a PPD outfit that made him look tough and confident.

Rudy was the first one over to look the android up and

down. "Whoa. This is amazing. Dude looks like a Ken doll."

Petey said, "No, Ken dolls are smooth down there." He was pointing at Rusty's groin. "This guy's got the CommandoCock 300 or SuperSchlong 150 or whatever."

"It's the ExtendoPackage 1000," Madison corrected him.

"Yeah, that," affirmed Petey.

Jin gave her a sour look. She didn't seem to mind.

"Is he fully functional?" he asked.

"I haven't had a chance to try him out yet," replied Madison, "but I would assume he could please me without—"

"Sorry, no," Jin quickly intercepted her explanation before she could get much further. "I'm talking about his ability with weapons."

"Dude," Petey said, still pointing, "that thing *is* a weapon."

"Guns," Jin stated evenly. "Guns, knives, explosives, hand-to-hand combat, and so on. Those are the things I'm talking about, people. Those are the *only* things I'm talking about."

While giving Jin a deadpan stare—one that felt almost as if the android was challenging him—Rusty said, "I am more than capable in the realm of combat, Chief Kannon."

Jin tilted his head. There was definitely some tension there. Would Rusty respond to everyone in the same manner or was his attitude reserved for Jin? And, if so, why?

He shook his head, realizing that if the android *did* have some kind of problem with him, it'd have to wait.

The zombies were the priority. The PPD was here to protect the city of San Diego and as long as Jin Kannon remained the chief of the precinct he was going to his damndest to make sure that happened.

"I know each of you has a different perspective on how we might manage this challenge," he began, looking from face to face. "I'm pretty sure everyone can agree that I don't have the same knowledge of this area that each of you carries, but what I *can* bring to this team is the mindset of an assassin." Their ears perked up at that. "I have special skills here, so let me get into some of how I think we should manage this. If anything clicks, we'll use it; if not, we'll let it go. Agreed?"

Everyone nodded, except for Rusty. He just continued his ornery stare.

It was strange, but Jin had seen worse. Of course, he'd never faced down an android before, so maybe he hadn't actually seen worse.

Again, he let it go.

"The first thing I'll say is that I'd never go in to fight an army head-on. Now, I was always on single-person missions, so it's not quite the same thing. Regardless, I would carefully plan each step in order to bypass the majority of the army. That way I'd get to the people I needed to get to without making a racket along the way." He sighed. "The problem is, we don't know who the main guy is, right?"

Raina raised his hand. "I would guess it's Emiliano."

Jin shot a quick look over at Hector. He was nodding in agreement.

"Based on the circumstances, he does seem to be the

most logical suspect," agreed Jin. "Assuming that is the case, in my experience, the boss always heads to their main lair. This is particularly true if they're planning to attack someone or if they believe they're going to be attacked."

"Is there a third option?" asked Rusty with an edge.

Jin raised an eyebrow. "That they're not attacking or being attacked?"

Rusty glanced around, blinking a few times. "Oh, right."

"My father—or whatever he is now—is definitely going to end up back in one of the cartel's compounds. I would imagine the main one." He gestured toward Jin. "That's the place we met. Anyway, we've already seen zombies are there now, so it's only a matter of time before he returns and takes over."

Jin nodded at him. "Exactly. So, if we can safely assume he'll be at the main compound, we can come up with a tactic to attack him."

"There's a tunnel system," offered Cano, which garnered him shocked looks from the other three. "What? The boss said we were supposed to work with the PPD, so that's what I'm doing."

Hector dropped his evil stare. "You're right, Cano. I'm sorry." He sighed. "My father taught me some things a little *too* well, I'm afraid."

Madison snapped her fingers, which immediately caused Rusty to drop to one knee and bow his head. Everyone gave him a sour look, even though they were keenly aware of why he'd gone into his submissive stance. As for Madison, she merely rolled her eyes.

"What if we don't attack immediately," she suggested. "Instead, sneak into each of the compounds, install surveillance cameras and microphones, and get back out. We'll be able to know what's going on, figure out schedules—if zombies do that sort of thing—and just get the lay of the land."

"Smart," Jin said, causing Rusty to give him a harsh glance and a sneer.

Odd.

Madison clearly hadn't noticed the android's attitude. "I have built tech they won't be able to see, too." She was standing proudly. "We'll be like ghosts in the wall."

Catching that everyone else in the room was nodding, aside from Rusty, of course, Jin nodded as well.

"Sounds perfect," he said. "Like I said, the more information we have before making a move, the better. Everyone get set up, load up the tech, and let's get our butts in gear."

He was about to ask Rusty in for a quick one-on-one chat, in order to see what was going on with him, but the android had already followed Madison back out of the room like a puppy hoping for a treat.

That was *not* something Jin wanted to visualize.

CHAPTER 14

Vestin

*H*e decided to take a few minutes to speak with Carina. The witch had been mostly kept to the side as everything was being set up, but that would change soon. Plus, while he had been pretty harsh with the woman before, he wanted to show her his gentler side. It was yet another skill taught in vampire schools in the Netherworld. Vestin preferred his heavy-handed methods, of course, but he wasn't stupid enough to look the other way when good advice was given.

Both Emiliano and Prender hadn't been summoned, but they showed up anyway.

Prender looked a bit green. Literally. His flesh held the appearance of a man who had recently taken ill.

"Are you unwell, Prender?"

"No, My Lord," he replied. "It's just that earlier I...I..."

"I shat upon him," Emiliano explained.

Vestin sat straight up at that admission. "You did what?"

"I had a momentary lapse of judgment, My Lord," said Emiliano, "whereby I considered reaching for more power than you have granted me."

"Ah." Vestin relaxed. "I see. Well, I suppose you've learned your lesson?"

"I have, My Lord," answered Emiliano, looking more than a bit relieved. "Should I ever get backed up due to eating too much cheese—or, I suppose eating a person who's had too much cheese, since I'm a zombie now—I can simply think about taking over your job and I'll be cleared out in no time."

Vestin frowned at the man. It was *not* the lesson he'd hoped Emiliano would glean, but it was also irrelevant. The point was that his lead zombie, and also anyone else who served under Vestin's venom, was incapable of attempting to usurp him.

He leaned toward Carina. "I hope at least *you* see the effects of my powers here?"

She was holding her nose. "I *smell* the effects of your power here."

Was a little respect honestly too much to ask? Vestin already knew the answer to that, and it drove him back to the point of having his conversation with her. He recalled his professor's words. "There will be times when your bite may be ineffective. When this happens—and fool yourself not, for it shall—it will be your words that demand fealty. Failing that, rely on the delivery of pain. Subjugation may take many forms, in fact. Alas, study after study has demonstrated the most successful tactic has proven to be securing a willing participant. In short, while it may be a personal affront, your most loyal subjects outside of your bite will be those who genuinely respect you."

And that was the problem. In all of his years, Vestin could think of no one who genuinely respected him. Even his parents had considered him "a vile little creature." Originally, he'd taken that as a compliment, until he grew to understand their actual meaning. He got the last laugh on them when he proved their words were factual. Somehow, through no fault of his, of course, they'd both fallen into a wood chipper. Vestin could still recall that delicious day as his parents were turned into mulch.

That's when he recognized Carina was staring at him with worry.

"Why are you looking at me like that?" she asked. "It's creepy." She shivered. "It's like you want to throw me into a wood chipper or something."

"A wood chipper?" Could she read his mind? Even peripherally? That would *not* be good. "Why would you think that?"

"Maybe because you were mouthing the words 'wood chipper' while staring at me?"

Damn.

"Oh! No, no, no." He waved his hands and forced himself to chuckle slightly. "I was thinking it *would* be great if Carina and I could be more *chipper* with each other. I guess I compressed the two words. I *do* have a fast mind, after all, and I find that my mouth sometimes struggles to keep up with it." It was weak, but explaining the whole thing about what he'd actually been thinking would've soured the entire plan. He quickly pushed on. "I know that when you arrived, I was far less than pleasant and I want to…apologize."

That hurt.

It also caused Prender and Emiliano to snap their heads up in disbelief. Prender was easy to manipulate because he was incredibly weak. Emiliano was under Vestin's venom, making him naturally submissive. His stomach issues had proven that. But they were still both quite capable of understanding that a tyrannical leader rarely used a gentle touch with peons.

He had to thread his way through this facade carefully.

"These two idiots," he stated, motioning at the two men, "are barely capable of tying their own shoelaces without a guidebook." Their bodies slumped again. Perfect. "You, however, clearly have capabilities beyond the norm."

She appeared both flattered and concerned.

"Now, I *could* continue using threats against you, followed by dire pain, but I would much prefer not to resort to such measures." That wasn't true at all. "Therefore, I shall simply suggest that we find a common ground whereby you willingly do what is needed of you. In return, you shall be treated well, provided wonderful meals, wines, a nice place to live, and even gifts."

Carina put her hands on her hips and gave him a look. "Wait, are you wanting me to do magic for you or are you expecting me to bed you down on a regular basis?"

Vestin sat back at her words, frowning furiously. What

in the devil was she talking about? He had no intention of…

"Ah," he said, finally grasping what he believed she'd gathered from his offer. "I assure you, madam, that while I'm certain there are many who may consider you attractive, you are not my type."

"Thank goodness," she mumbled.

Vestin frowned. "Thank goodness, indeed." He sniffed derisively and adjusted his sleeves. "Again, I'm sorry you saw it that way, but no. This is purely an employee-employer relationship."

Carina sighed and dropped her hands to her sides. "Fine."

He leaned forward again. "Does that mean you'll do it?"

"Yeah, sure. It's not like I have any better offers at the moment."

He would have preferred a higher level of enthusiasm, but it *was* better than what he'd anticipated. Vestin would take the win and move on.

"Excellent, because—"

He stopped at the sound of pattering feet.

A group of very odd-looking creatures walked into the room, causing everyone to take a step back. Vestin couldn't step back, though it did take everything in his power to not lift his feet up and curl them under himself.

The image of the creatures before him was the thing of nightmares.

They were essentially dogs but with human-like faces. They were still hairy and had pointed ears, though, which served to further the disturbing visage. The rest of their bodies were normal, as far as dogs went. It was just those damned faces. Worse, their cheeks, chins, and foreheads were completely devoid of hair, aside from their eyebrows anyway. It was almost as if regular dog hair framed their otherwise smooth faces.

"What the hell are you?" blurted Emiliano.

One of the things moved forward and looked up at the large zombie. Vestin could hardly fault Emiliano for taking yet another step away.

"Ah, Emiliano," the "dog" said, "I wondered if this day would ever come. My mother warned me to stay away from you at all costs, but I knew it'd only be a matter of time before our paths finally crossed."

"You know this...thing?" asked Vestin.

Emiliano shook his head in horror. "Never seen it in my life."

"First off, I am not a 'thing.' I am a werecoyote and have a name. It's Einstein."

Everyone, except for the other coyotes said, "Einstein?"

"Correct." He then turned around and nodded at the others in his flock. "These are my brothers: Rex, Spot, Rover, and Lightbulb." He spun back and again focused his attention on Emiliano. "It's only fitting that a father knows the names of his sons."

The sound of silence in the room at that moment actually hurt Vestin's ears.

Carina began to laugh. "Wow. I knew you were a major horndog, Emiliano, but I never thought you'd be dumb enough to have sex with a coyote." She slapped her knee. "I hope you were at least in werewolf form when it happened." She laughed harder when Vestin's face contorted even more. "Don't worry, Vestin, he *had* to have been in werewolf form. I was just joking. He couldn't have procreated with a coyote otherwise."

"Ah. Still...ew."

"I don't remember this at all," Emiliano stated in a huff. "I mean, I don't really remember much about the times I was a werewolf, especially when it came to sexing, but a coyote?"

"We have pictures of you and our mother," said Einstein as a swirl of magic surrounded him.

He morphed a few moments later, but all that happened was his torso became bare, sporting two shiny nipple rings and his front legs turned into human-like arms, including an overly large set of hands and fingers. It was seriously creepy.

Reaching into the little pack he had fastened around his waist, Einstein pulled out a number of printed pictures. It was hard to know if Vestin was actually seeing Emiliano in those photos because he'd never seen him in werewolf mode before. Fortunately, it seemed Carina *had* seen him before and she confirmed it was indeed him.

"Yep," she said, "he has the telltale skunk stripe going across his forehead..." She paused and pointed at the coyotes. "All of them have it, too. Smaller, sure, but it's definitely there."

Sure enough, they *did* have the same markings, where there was hair.

Emiliano put his back against the wall and slowly slid down, looking completely shocked.

"I had no idea," he said, shaking his head. "I've had

many trysts over the years, but…" He looked back up at them. "I had no idea. I'm truly sorry. Truly, truly sorry."

That seemed to soften the glare on Einstein's face.

"If I had only known…"

"Yes?" asked Einstein hopefully as the other coyotes leaned in with upturned faces.

"I would've killed you all immediately."

They all let out sad sighs.

"Right," said Einstein. "Well, I suppose we should have expected that." He put the pictures away and morphed back into his "normal" self, turning his attention to Vestin. "Anyway, we recognize that you are looking to take over the town and we would like to assist. Our lives have been challenging, as you may imagine, and we feel that if we were to aid you in your fight, we could garner at least some measure of respect in this world."

Vestin considered it for a moment. Honestly, he could probably utilize these little monsters to drive people out of town just by looking at them. But knowing they were part werewolf and part coyote could also mean he could zombify them and make them into something huge, ugly, *and* mean. That would be even better.

"Fine," he said, nodding toward Prender. "Give them the venom."

"Me?" Prender said, a look of terror in his eyes. "I don't want to go near those things, My Lord!"

"It wasn't a request, Prender."

"It doesn't matter anyway," Einstein interrupted. "You see, you probably don't remember this, but my mom told a story about some vampire asshole who bit her while she was about halfway through her gestation. The dick-fluffering, fanged-fiend was unsuccessful, though. Based on your face, which my mother described in detail, and your flowery scent, which she passed along to us, we know it was you."

Vestin had bitten hundreds of animals over the years as he'd worked on perfecting his venom, so he was certain it had indeed been him, though he disagreed with the flowery scent comment...and the part about him being a dick-fluffering, fanged-fiend, too.

"Anyway," continued Einstein, "you may certainly try your venom on us if you wish, but my assumption is that we all have a natural immunity against your bite that was built into our DNA due to your carelessness."

They would, indeed. It was one of the struggles with doing testing. Anyone who had not become infected during his initial trials would have built up effective antibodies to protect them. In other words, his earlier attempts were essentially vaccines.

Still, it was worth a try.

"Prender," he said, pointing at Einstein, "now."

"But, boss—"

Carina pushed off the wall and walked over to Vestin's second-in-command and held out her hand. "Give me the syringe, you wuss. I'll do it."

She took it from him and kneeled down, jabbing the needle into the coyote's back leg. It grimaced as she pressed down the plunger, but made no sound.

The latest version of Vestin's venom could drop a man within ten seconds. The coyote was still standing, blinking at him, after thirty seconds had passed.

"As you can see," Einstein ultimately said, "it doesn't

affect us. Knowing that we are *still* here to help you in return for a small area to rule over when all is said and done."

Ruling an area? No. What could five ugly coyotes do for him anyway? Again, except for scaring people away for a time. They had to bring more to the table than that if they were to make demands. But maybe they harbored something he *could* use and he just couldn't see it. And even if they were capable of bringing something to aid in his quest, would it be possible for Vestin to stomach looking at the horrible creatures during their weekly meetings? The thought made bile rise up in his throat.

There were worse things Vestin would need to tolerate in order to be king and *far* worse things for him to remain so. If Einstein, Rex, Rover, Spot, and Lightbulb were able to aid in that quest, it would be remiss of him to ignore it simply because they were a collective horror to look at.

With some effort, he asked, "What can you do for me?"

"We are excellent with information gathering," Einstein replied. "We can type over one hundred words per minute, we have perfect memories, and we're great cuddlers."

"Ew," Vestin said, his face etched in disgust, but he was thankful to hear they weren't capable of providing anything he could get from more attractive animals. "I think we'll pass on your offer."

"That would be a mistake," Einstein warned.

"Oh?"

"We have no problem turning against you and helping the PPD instead."

Vestin considered that for a moment. Would it really

matter to him if the PPD learned who he was, what he was doing, and any other details they could gather from the coyotes? It could've put a dent in his plans if they'd arrived months ago, but with his zombie army growing and his plan to unleash the venom on the masses very soon, he found himself less than worried.

Besides, he couldn't imagine the members of the PPD stomaching having to look at these things for long, either.

"Oh, you should absolutely do that," he said, trying his best to hold in his mirth. "I can't imagine a better fate... erm...*find* for our paranormal police pals."

Einstein glared at him and gritted his teeth. "You've just made an enemy of us, Turd Vestin."

Vestin jolted. "That's *Lord* Vestin."

"Not to me, it isn't."

"Seize them," Vestin commanded a few of the zombie guards. "If they want to play this game, we'll simply burn them alive and be done with their horrid little faces."

The zombies took a step toward the coyotes but abruptly stopped as the dogs all morphed into their sort-of-human forms and pulled forth knives. Obviously, the zombies weren't afraid of the weapons, but they each looked disgusted at the prospect of having to touch the little beasts.

"Go on, fight!" commanded Vestin, using a voice that boomed his demand.

The zombies shook their heads and then began to double over, grabbing their stomachs as their weapons clanked on the ground. Within seconds, shit shot against the far walls, proving yet again that Vestin's venom was powerful. Maybe a bit *too* powerful.

The coyotes laughed, put their blades away, and morphed back into their "normal" selves.

"Pathetic," Einstein said to Vestin as he and his crew walked out of the room, unscathed. Though the one they called "Lightbulb" stopped for a moment, lifted his leg, and marked the wall by the door.

CHAPTER 15

Jin

Jin had taken Raina and Hector along with him as the teams split up. It was smarter to cover multiple properties at once, especially if they happened to get caught. Better just a few of them than the entire squad.

They were in the tunnels that connected to the main house belonging to *The Dogs*, or more likely the zombies now. They'd elected to go to the main house because it was the only one Hector had familiarity with when it came to the tunnels. His guards knew about all of the different layouts, but it was apparently still new to Hector.

Based on what little Jin knew about the man, he seemed decent enough, as far as mob bosses went, at least. That didn't mean Hector was a good guy. It was still too early in their relationship to make that determination, but, again, he *seemed* okay. It was kind of surprising when you put it into the context of having been raised by the likes of Emiliano, the guy everyone considered to be quite the asshole. For Hector to not even know about the escape tunnels was telling enough. To even *consider* not letting your own child know how to get out of the compound in the event of an attack? That was crazy to Jin.

"I get the feeling you're worried about going into the tunnels, chief," Raina said through their connection. *"I'm a little nervous about it, too. Tight spaces and unicorns aren't exactly a good combination."*

"I was actually thinking about Hector's situation, Raina."

"Oh, I'm sure he's fine with being in the tunnels. He's a werewolf. They're used to living in dens and stuff."

Jin closed his eyes for a moment. *"No, I meant his situation with his father."*

"Ah! Right. Yeah, Emiliano was a real piece of work." She paused. *"I suppose he still is, but now his personality better matches his appearance."*

"Yeah, I would imagine." Jin shrugged. *"Anyway, regarding you being concerned about tight spaces, you're more than welcome to stay behind. I completely understand."*

"You're claustrophobic, too?"

He moved his head about noncommittally. *"I don't like tight spaces, but I've had to build strategies over the years in order to tolerate them. Kind of goes with the job I held."* Memories sprang forth, proving to him that the integration had been successfully reversed, at least as far as his recollections were concerned. *"The worst was when I had to sit in a sealed barrel for ten hours, having only a single hole that served as both a peephole and a pee hole."*

"Ew."

"Agreed. Fortunately, it'd been cold out so it didn't get too hot in there. Unfortunately, the coldness made it difficult to 'hang' myself out of that hole very far when nature called."

Raina said nothing in response as they entered the main tunnel area. She was just in front of Jin, her hands pressing against the walls as if trying to keep them at bay.

"Seriously, Raina, you don't have to do this. Head back out while we're still close and it'll be fine."

"I can't do that, chief," she replied, but it was ragged. "If I'm ever going to get beyond deputy, I have to be able to do things like this. What kind of boss makes their teams do stuff they won't do, you know?"

Jin imagined most of them did, but he kept that to himself.

"Okay, Raina, here's something that may help. One time I had to go through a tunnel that was much smaller than this. It was about a half-mile long, too. Anyway, what I did was count my moves so I would know precisely how many I needed to make in order to get back out. If you count your steps, that may help so your mind can't imagine the trek is longer than it truly is."

She was nodding as he spoke, clearly unaware that she was saying her count through the connection. Jin didn't mind. Honestly, knowing that information was good, regardless of any fear of enclosed spaces. If they had to get out of the tunnel in a jiffy, it would be nice to know exactly how far they had to move.

When she hit one hundred and nineteen, the tunnel opened up into a cavern.

Hector stopped at the opening until Raina pushed past

him and took in a huge breath of air, putting her arms directly above her head before slowly moving them down in an arc until they were at her sides. She did this a few times as Hector looked at Jin in confusion.

"Claustrophobia," Jin whispered, trying to be discrete.

The mob boss gave him one of those "Ah" looks and then pointed ahead. "Those are all much larger than what we went through. I'm assuming you want to get to the room where my father will be staying?"

"I'm guessing anyplace we can put these cameras, or whatever they are, would be useful."

"Well, that one leads to the main living area and that one goes to the men's showers. I'm sure it's not necessary to put any in there."

Madison may have felt differently, but Jin agreed. "Just the places where people gather to talk, then."

"Right." Hector walked forward. "That'll be up in the main office and the living room." He stopped and checked his watch. "Okay, good."

"What's good?" asked Raina, who had rejoined them. She looked a lot better, proving certain levels of enclosure weren't as bad as others.

"Father only goes into his office at certain times," Hector replied. "It should be empty right now, unless he's changed the way he does things as a zombie, of course."

If so, Jin would have to kill Emiliano and that would set in motion the wheels falling off of the zombie empire. He believed that would be the case, anyway. Most of the time there was one major douchebag running these things. They would rise up the ranks spewing garbage, sewing discord, and cracking heads wherever possible. Everyone else would slowly fall into line, like a bunch of mindless cowards. Any group of them could band together and destroy the leader, but they rarely did so unless there was some path to greater glory, or, more likely, there was an even bigger ass maggot sitting around waiting to take the reins.

Either way, Jin knew his skills and there were very few people alive who could even come close to matching them. Now, granted, Emiliano *wasn't* alive in the traditional sense, but that didn't make him a better fighter. Stronger, certainly. Jin still recalled how powerful the guy had been during their first encounter. That was irrelevant in the face of bullets, though, and Jin's guns were deadly accurate.

"Let's go to the office," he said. "If Emiliano is in there, you'll just need to wait outside for a few minutes."

Hector swallowed hard and nodded. "If you're sure."

"I'm sure."

Three corners later they found themselves peeking into a completely empty office. If Jin was being honest, he would've said it was a bit of a letdown. The one thing he'd perfected was killing off bosses. But he *did* have a standard way of managing the process and this wasn't it. Still, to have nipped the problem in the bud here and now would have been great. No, it wouldn't have ended the zombies outright, but it was much easier to destroy an army without a leader, so having Emiliano out of the way would certainly have been a plus.

Instead, the threesome set about putting up the tech Madison had provided.

"Are you getting this, Madison?" asked Raina through a shared connection.

"Perfectly. You're the first ones to set up, but I'm assuming you'll be tagging other areas of the house?"

"That's the plan," answered Jin. *"I think we're only going to be gaining access to one other room, though."*

"Hmmm," said Madison. *"I thought certain I'd heard Sofia say there were three tunnels."*

"There are," Jin answered. *"This office and the main living area are the only two we'll be tagging."*

"Hmmm. I took notes here and Sofia said one of the tunnels led to the men's showers. We should really be sure to put a number of cameras in there."

"I can't see how that would help," Jin replied as he shook his head at Raina.

"It'd help me," Madison pointed out. *"On top of that, I'm sure there's loads of information that could be gleaned by checking out packages."*

Jin sighed, wondering if he should add that to his list of cons or not. *"You do recall these guys are all zombies now, right? That means the likelihood of them showering is quite low, and even if they did, do you seriously want to look at zombie packages?"*

"Okay, fair enough. While I am a fan of trying almost anything once, I think zombies would be a hard no even for me."

"Swell. We'll hit you back up when we're done with the living room."

"Sounds good."

Madison disconnected the call and Jin glanced over at Raina. She was smiling to herself, but that's all Jin needed to see to know she'd been enjoying the conversation between him and Madison.

"Is she always that warped?" he asked, already knowing the answer.

"I don't kink-shame, chief," she replied. "I'd say 'warped' comes in various shapes and sizes. Maybe you're just a bit of a prude?"

That stung a little, but she wasn't wrong.

"Yeah," he answered with a sigh, "maybe I am."

They headed back the way they came and then took the next tunnel over. This one led to the living area. There was a single zombie in there who appeared to have fallen asleep while reading a magazine. He was sitting in a lounge chair that was kicked back. His feet were up and he was snoring something fierce.

Jin put his finger to his lips and motioned for the others to stay put. He then slipped into the room and began placing the devices everywhere he could reach, making sure they were tucked away enough to not be seen while also ensuring they could catch ample video and sound.

As he stepped back after sticking one piece on a shelf behind the sleeping monster, he bumped into the chair.

"Fnork," it said, jolting slightly. "What was that?"

Jin stayed perfectly still, holding his breath. He had no problem killing the guy, but if they could get out without anyone knowing they'd been there, that would be a better scenario. It was always best to go unseen during this phase of the job.

The zombie yawned, though it sounded like a whirlwind of hate. He then stretched out and moved around a bit on the chair, grunting more than anyone ever should. Finally, he settled down and within seconds, he was back to his rhythmic snoring.

Moving even more carefully than before, Jin crept back out of the room.

"That was close," Raina whispered.

"Tell me about it." He then gave her a look. "You ready to go back through the tunnel and get out of here?"

She nodded. "One hundred and nineteen steps."

CHAPTER 16

Rudy

*R*udy had suggested that he and Clive go to the main house, originally, but Raina said that'd be a bad idea since it was where he'd had his "run-in" with Dr. Ty Sanchez.

He disagreed, thinking that bumping into the one-fingered bandit again would be great, but that was only because he wanted to punch the guy in the nads.

Okay, so maybe it wouldn't have been such a grand plan. They were supposed to be incognito. Beating the piss out of the veterinarian from hell would probably draw more attention than they needed at the time. At some point, though, Rudy planned to get even. *Not* by doing the same thing to the doctor that the doctor had done to him, of course. That would be…ew. But there were more "normal" ways to get even.

Rudy, Clive, and Sofia entered the tunnel of the Rankor House, which was considered the second most strategic location for *The Dogs*. They moved into the shadows at the sound of footsteps up ahead.

"Who's that?" whispered Clive. "Can't be a zombie, unless they've found some exceedingly large dress shoes to wear."

The clicking sound of those footfalls did resemble the tick-tack echo of heels on concrete. They weren't thin heels. The sound was too full, too deep. Spikes tended to be very sharp in pitch, whereas the larger, rounded heel, gave off almost a "clunk" sound.

Sofia was leaning out just far enough so she could catch sight of who it was.

Then she stepped away from the shadows. "Hey, doc," she said. "Trying to hide out in the tunnels, too?"

His face registered shock and then he reached for his armband.

Rudy leapt out and punched the dude in the side of the head, dropping him instantly and leaving him on the ground completely out. He wasn't going to lie, it felt good. It felt *really* good. It wasn't enough to sate his desire for revenge, but it wasn't awful either.

"What the hell did you do that for?" Sofia hissed, punching Rudy on the bicep.

"He was going for something," Rudy replied, rubbing his arm with a wince.

"Yeah," she agreed, pointing at the doctor's arm, "his voice device, you dipshit."

Clive was shaking his head at Rudy. "You punched him because he fingered your ass without taking you to dinner first."

"I was in rooster mode!"

Sofia reached over and put her hand across Rudy's mouth, staring anger into his eyes.

"Keep your voice down, you fucking idiot. You *do* remember there are zombies everywhere, right?" She leaned closer, squeezing his face until he grunted. "Right?"

Rudy nodded and Sofia let go.

"*She's mean,*" he said through the connector to Clive.

"*And you're stupid. Yelling in here? Really? Are you* trying *to get us killed?*"

"*You're stupid,*" grumped Rudy.

"*Good comeback, finger puppet.*"

Just as he was about to launch back his best retort, a growling voice from upstairs called out, "Who's down there?"

"Why you think somebody's down there, Sally?" asked another voice.

"Cause I heard something, Carl," she replied. "I mean, honestly, why else would I think someone is down here? Do you think I have some kind of clairvoyance ability now that I'm in this horror show of a body?"

There was a pause, followed by Carl saying, "I think you look just as pretty as ever, I do."

"You do?"

Rudy, Clive, and Sofia glanced at each other, assuming Carl had nodded his reply. It was difficult to imagine anyone thinking of a zombie as pretty, but maybe once you got zombified you ended up with a different take on beauty. Rudy never had a thing for chickens when in his human form—thankfully—but when he turned into a rooster, it took a lot of effort to keep him away from even the homeliest in the bunch.

"Huh," said Sally. "Well, Carl, I have to admit that when we were simply werewolves, you kind of grossed me out, but as a zombie, you're...rugged."

"I am?"

"You are." There was a rustling sound. "Let's go up to the bedroom and destroy each other. What do you say?"

"Hell yeah," Carl replied.

It was disturbing to imagine, so Rudy started thinking about something else. Unfortunately, the first place he looked was down at Dr. Sanchez, who was gazing back up at him while blinking in confusion. The doctor's dismay faded quickly and he grinned.

Clive grabbed Rudy and pulled him away before he could punch the guy again.

"But he's taunting me!"

"No, he's not. He just smiled because he saw another face."

"You don't know that, Clive!"

"Actually, you fart-scented penis, I do. Just think it through logically. Did he see you after *fingering your ass when you were a chicken?"*

Rudy snarled. *"A ROOSTER, you titty pube! And, no, he didn't see me in my normal form. I think."*

"Then how would he know it was you?"

That question stopped Rudy in his tracks. Clive was right. How *would* the human rectal thermometer know it was him? Maybe Rudy *was* being ridiculous. If the doctor thought he was an actual rooster, then maybe the whole thing was just normal practice for him. Could it be that the guy was just doing what vets do and it was all in the name of health?

Ugh.

Now he felt bad.

So, he turned back to offer a hand in helping the doctor back to his feet.

That's when he saw the doc with a finger under his nose, still glancing up at Rudy, but now his eyebrows were wiggling in a flirty way.

"That's it!"

Clive had to tackle Rudy before he got to the doctor, and also before Sofia got to Rudy. There was no doubt Rudy was going to pummel the doctor for teasing about the finger stuff and it was clear Sofia was going to pummel Rudy for making so much noise.

"Hey," called down a different voice from upstairs, "is somebody down there?"

"What's your problem, Gary?" asked another voice. "I ain't hearing anything."

"That's cause you're deaf, Rich."

"I am not!"

"You are so!"

There was the sound of scuffling and grunting. They were clearly having a fight at the top of the stairs. It lasted a solid minute before finally stopping.

"You wanna go to the bedroom, Rich?"

"What?"

"YOU WANNA GO TO THE BEDROOM?"

"Oh! Yeah!"

They shuffled away as the others all looked at each other in amazement.

"Are you sure we're at Rankor House?" asked Clive. "Seems more like the Love Shack."

Sofia glanced up and to the left, considering the

question. Then she shrugged and whispered, "Most of them are like this, actually. You tend to get a lot of sexual tension when you're fighting alongside people, you know?"

Clive gave Rudy a sideways glance. "I really don't."

"Nice," Rudy said, and then he gave the middle finger to Doctor Sanchez, who smiled back and held up his index finger in response. "You mother—"

That was interrupted by a gut punch thrown by Sofia. It dropped Rudy to his knees as his eyes threatened to pop out of his head.

"We may not get lucky a third time, shithead," she growled as she dragged Dr. Sanchez to his feet. Then she wagged a finger at the doctor. "As for you, if you keep on teasing him about what happened, I'll let him whoop your ass."

The doctor lowered his hand and stopped smiling.

"Good," said Sofia. "Now, how many zombies are up there?"

Dr. Sanchez slowly pressed the button on his wristband and said, "Four." It sounded robotic, though the volume was low. "It's only Sally, Carl, Gary, and Rich. Are you here to save me?"

"Save him? SAVE HIM?"

"Chill, dude," Clive warned, *"unless you want Sofia to mop the floor with you."*

"We're here to...check on things," Sofia replied, sounding a bit guarded. She then pointed at Clive. "He's going to stay down here with you while me and Rudy go upstairs to survey everything." She turned to Clive. "One wrong move and you have my authorization to kill him. Just make it quiet."

"Hey," Rudy rasped, "why can't *I* kill him?"

"Because you'll kill him for no reason at all," Sofia pointed out.

"I would say I've got a pretty good reason."

The doctor rolled his eyes and pressed the button on his wrist again. "Look, I'm sorry I teased you just now. It was unprofessional of me. If I had known you were a wererooster, I would never have given you such a thorough exam…at least not without getting your consent first."

He seemed genuine.

"It's true," Sofia stated. "We get our checkups by him all the time. Nobody likes that particular part of the exam…" She paused. "Okay, *some* people like it, but that's not the point. He only does it because it's his job."

"Except for doing it with those who actually enjoy it," the Doctor admitted. "Otherwise, it's purely clinical." He then frowned. "But sometimes people get really riled up at me and my default is to tease them." He looked at Rudy once more. "Again, that's wrong of me and I know it, so I *do* apologize. But please note when I'm doing the examination it's one hundred percent professional."

Rudy eyed him for a moment. "You're being for real with me right now?"

The doctor wiggled his eyebrows again. "As far as you know."

Sofia landed another punch before Rudy could make his move.

CHAPTER 17

Lacey

*L*acey was amazed that Chimi had been able to squeeze through the tunnel. It wasn't a problem for Lacey, obviously, but she rarely found herself in situations where she'd been incapable of moving. That came with the territory of being a leprechaun. There were a few negatives too, of course, such as people constantly picking her up and demanding she grant them wishes, but for the most part, she was just another magic user who happened to also be excellent with miniature weapons. She did enjoy granting the occasional wish, especially when the person demanding it of her was a total tool about it. Her favorite was the guy who'd commanded her to give him a bigger dick than the one he had. She shrugged and complied, only not as he'd been expecting. He got the last laugh, though, having ended up becoming a huge porn star who'd acted in features such as *Foreskin Forehead*, *Dong Noggin'*, and *Boner Brow*.

She recalled seeing an interview with him only a couple of weeks back...

∿

"His name is Richard McTuggins," said Candy Whaddarack, "which may simply be a stage name, unlike mine, and he's starred in more adult films than any other male actor over the last five years."

The camera panned out and showed the image of a smiling man who had a rather large appendage dangling just past his nose. He also had a major combover, which was half curly hair and half straight. He coughed and the tip of the monster moved ever so slightly.

"So, Mr. McTuggins," Candy started and then stopped. "Actually, may I call you Richard?"

"Dick, please."

"Funny, I say that all the time." She cleared her throat...also something she did often. "Anyway, you claim to be from Nantucket. Is that true or are you just playing off the old limerick?"

"We'll leave that as a mystery," he laughed as his head-johnson flopped around. "Actually," he added, pushing his dong out of the way as if he were just correcting his hairstyle, "you can find the answer to that in chapter 37 of my book."

"Hopefully there's an audiobook version because I'm not what you may call a 'reader.'" There was no reply. "Right. So, of all the films you have acted in, including

Fuckhead, Fuck Face, Ouch...My Pounding Head, Keepin'
Your Eyes On Your Balls, Cock Cranium, Mind Fuck—one
and two, *I Sneeze To Please, Dew North, Snoggin' Noggin,*
Head Horn Hysteria, Knob Nose, Full Frontal Fuckstick, Head
Honcho, Crosseyed Beef Whistle, Vein Brain, Cockeyed,
Crowning Glory: The Legend of Phallus Forehead, Peen on
the Scene, Third-Eye Throbbin', Skull Shaft Shenanigans,
Pride and Priapisms, Blue Balls & Black Eyes, Temple
Tappers, Stiff Up-Her Lip, and, of course, your most
famous of all, *Full Jizz A-Head,* which of those was *your*
favorite?"

"You'll find the answer to that in chapter 23."

Candy sighed at him. "Man, you really want people to
buy this book, don't ya?" She then reached for a card and
held it up. "Okay, so we have a question from one of our
viewers. Are you able to self-pleasure now?"

Dick frowned, which looked super strange with his
flopper bouncing off his nose. "No. Not really, anyway. I
mean, I can get started, but once I get aroused, it goes up
and I can't reach it again." He shrugged. "On the plus side,
if I'm horny and I tie a bit of aluminum foil to the tip and
put my hand on the TV, we get great reception."

"Ohhhhhhkay," said Candy. "Well, that's all the time we
have for now. Be sure you catch all of Dick McTuggins'
films and pick up his autobiography entitled *Dickhead* at
your local Chick-Fil-A in the 'burned books' section."

The smell of stew struck them as they got to the main
tunnel alcove. Lacey's stomach growled at the scent.

While she was more of a sausage and sauerkraut kind of girl, the spices filling the air were calling to her hunger.

"Ah," said Cano, a look of serenity on his face. "Man, I love this place. The chef here makes such wonderful food." He gave them both a sour look. "Unfortunately, he only makes stew, which gets kind of old after a while, but it's been a while since the last time I've had it, and a bowl or two sounds pretty damn good right now."

"Amen," agreed Lacey.

"We have to work," Chimi pointed out. "We're not here for stew or for talking about stew, remember?"

Lacey rolled her eyes. She and Cano were being rhetorical...maybe. The point is that everyone was well aware of what needed to be done, and it wasn't eating stew. It just irked Lacey when Chimi overstepped her position.

"We'll eat stew if I'm after sayin' we'll eat stew, *Sergeant*," Lacey said, making it clear she wasn't going to be bullied by the bigger officer. It was unfair since Chimi would never even consider bullying anyone on the force, but Lacey still treated it that way. "Now, you happen to be on the right of it, but if anyone's gonna be after givin' orders around here, it's me, got it?"

"Sorry, Lacey," Chimi replied, her face instantly downcast. "I'm just trying to keep us on the mission."

The leprechaun recognized her surly attitude had gotten the better of her again. She was the rebellious sort who wasn't a fan of taking orders from bosses, let alone from her subordinates. That, however, gave her no right to be so grumpy with the likes of Chimi. The cyclops was as pure as a glittery unicorn turd, which are amazingly beautiful in an it-really-shouldn't-be kind of way.

"Bah! I'm the one who's after bein' sorry, Chimi. Yer in the right of it and I'm just a cantankerous sort is all."

Cano, who had been eyeing them both through their discourse, leaned in and said, "I appreciate how you two work out your differences. I do." He then motioned around at the three tunnels that Lacey assumed ran into the main house. "But if you could keep your voices down, we might actually make it out of this alive."

Lacey repeated her infamous, "Bah," only this time she whispered it.

They followed Cano through the center tunnel, which took them up to a large cafeteria. There were tables everywhere, but the only person working was the chef, and he wasn't a zombie.

"Jason," Cano said as he approached, only to find the chef spinning on him wicked fast with his chopping knife raised as if ready to attack. "Woah, man! It's me, Cano."

Jason lowered the blade and let out a relieved sigh. "You scared the shit out of me, dude. I've been so focused on this current batch of stew that I didn't hear you walk in." He scanned Chimi and Lacey. "Why are the cops here?"

"Because of the zombie stuff," answered Cano.

"What zombie stuff?"

Cano gave a look to Lacey and Chimi before explaining everything that had been going on. He even cited the details regarding how Hector had decided to work with the PPD. Jason seemed impressed by that.

"Wow," said the chef. "Man, I blocked way more out

than I thought. I haven't even left the kitchen in three days, except to use the facilities and grab a quick nap on that cot over there." He scratched the side of his head with the pommel of the knife. "Come to think of it, I'm just now realizing nobody's been in for a meal in quite a while."

"Yep."

"Huh. Well, goes to show you that when you're busting your hump on something, everything else just becomes background noise." Jason quickly pulled out three bowls and ladled a bit of stew in each. "Give this a taste, will ya?"

Lacey flittered down immediately and Cano wasn't shy about his desire to try out the new concoction either. Chimi was a bit more reserved, but even she hesitantly picked up the spoon and dipped it into the bowl of brown broth and veggies.

"Marry me," the cyclops said to Jason an instant later as her head snapped up.

He laughed.

Chimi's single eye stayed transfixed on the chef. "I'm not joking. Any man who can make this kind of meal may sire my children."

The laughter stopped. Jason swallowed hard. "Um... thanks, but I'm...uh...taken! Yes, that's it. I'm taken." He feigned sadness. "Such a shame, too, because *that*...um... officer...is a heckuva offer."

Honestly, the flavor profile of that stew caused Lacey to hear wedding bells also, but she kept that to herself. Still, the way he'd merged those spices, giving a comforting flavor with just a kick of heat was incredible. Why couldn't the PPD have a chef like this guy around?

"This is after bein' topnotch," she said in a wistful way, "but I believe it was me partner who pointed out we're here for doin' a job. And while me belly would rather stay and douse itself with a bucket full o' this stuff, we gotta be after gettin' to work."

Jason nodded and said, "Well, when you're done doing whatever you have to do, stop back by and I'll have a few containers built out that'll last you a few days."

It was all Lacey could do not to whimper.

They spread out in the cafeteria and got to work setting everything up. Lacey had the easiest time of it, since she could reach the high corners without a fuss. Fortunately, the tech given to them by Madison was pretty small, and the units had blending capabilities that allowed them to mimic the colors and shapes of the areas surrounding them. In other words, they were nearly impossible to see once they were installed. If there were anti-surveillance items at the disposal of *The Dogs*, however, Lacey assumed they'd sniff this stuff out in a jiffy. Then again, maybe not. These *were* devices created in Madison's workshop, and she was as devious as they came.

After finishing everything up, they slipped into the next room and the next, planting equipment as quickly as they could. There were no zombies anywhere to be seen, but that didn't mean they weren't going to show up sooner or later. With Lacey's luck, it'd be sooner.

"I'm out," Cano announced, showing the empty bag that'd previously held multiple cameras and listening devices.

"Me, too," agreed Chimi.

"Same," said Lacey. "Okay, let's get our moss-covered arses outta here."

"After picking up our to-go order first, right?" pleaded Cano.

"Yeah," agreed Chimi with some reluctance. "We wouldn't want to let Chef Jason down. His fiancé may dump him someday and I wouldn't want him to think of me poorly for leaving without taking the deliciously intoxicating food he'd promised."

Lacey squinted at her massive partner. "Riiiight. Wouldn't be after dreamin' of doin' anything that may cost ya a man, Chimi." She then flew in close and added, "And don't ye worry. I shan't be after lettin' Raffy know about yer interest in another."

She smiled devilishly to herself as she flew off, keeping the image of Chimi's shocked face fresh in her mind.

CHAPTER 18

Rusty

The android had been sent off alone with Alejandro. He assumed that was because, being an android, he needed no backup. Now, granted, should Alejandro have attacked Rusty from behind, all bets would've been off, but Rusty estimated the statistical likelihood of that happening as being less than one percent. That was only because of their current circumstances. If things had been as they typically were between the cartel and the PPD, that number would have been closer to fifty percent.

He knew that because it was his job to know.

While Rusty spent the majority of his time preoccupied with Mistress Kane, he was still required to keep current on the happenings in the precinct, the Paranormal Police Department as a whole, and the San Diego crime climate. With a mind like his, though, that took very little processing power.

The one thing that was digging into his chips at the moment, however, was Chief Jin Kannon. He was the new guy on the scene, yes, and he was also the new chief of the precinct, sure, but neither of those things bothered Rusty. What *did* bother him was how the chief had been speaking to Mistress Kane out on the beach. It would have been fine under normal circumstances, had Rusty not listened in on what was an intimate conversation. They'd shared things that his Mistress had never shared with him. At least Rusty felt no guilt over eavesdropping. One of Mistress' rules was that Rusty always listened in on her unless she explicitly told him not to. The only time she blocked him was when she was at one of the clubs she attended during certain evenings, and even that had been happening less and less as the months went on.

She'd not blocked him during her discussion with Chief Kannon, however, and he couldn't stop replaying their words over and over in his mind. There were parts of their conversation that made clear Rusty's Mistress was interested in the chief, and there was no doubt Kannon was interested right back.

Within microseconds, Rusty found himself growling.

"You okay, pal?" Alejandro asked, taking a step away from the android. "You look like you're about to overheat."

Rusty immediately launched a calming script and let out a long breath. While he didn't technically breathe, he knew it was something organics did so he copied it. He had to admit it *did* kind of help him relax further. Maybe that was in his coding?

"I think the new chief wants to bone Mistress Kane."

"Who doesn't?" laughed Alejandro. He then recognized Rusty's death stare and abruptly stopped. "I was just joking, pal. Seriously, though, you have to admit she's pretty hot."

Rusty dropped his ire again. "Don't I know it? I do everything I can to keep her happy and thinking of me, but I know she has eyes for other people."

"Well, she *is* a succubus, right?"

"Yeah, and I get that. I just wish it wasn't the case."

"Ouch."

The android glanced up, furrowing his brow while studying the guy. "Why did you say that?"

Alejandro started to speak a few times but kept stopping himself. He pointed twice at Rusty, yet still said nothing. Finally, he shrugged and let it out.

"Wishing somebody is something they aren't to have them be something *you* want them to be instead is kinda fucked up, man." His tone was almost admonishing. "Look, I get that you're like really into her and all that, but your statement is pretty damned selfish, and that's coming from me."

Rusty frowned further. Was there something about Alejandro that he was missing? The man seemed like your standard ruffian. He was big, brash, covered with tattoos and scars, and carried himself like someone who was ever anxious to get into a brawl.

The way he was speaking at the moment confused Rusty, though. Was he more sensitive than he appeared?

"What do you mean, Alejandro?"

The burly man hedged a few more times before saying, "It's just that I've lost plenty of nice ladies due to my

JOHN P. LOGSDON & JENN MITCHELL

jealousy issues. I tighten my grip on them so much that they end up doing the one thing I'm most afraid of them doing."

"Leave?"

"Leave," Alejandro affirmed. He then reached out and put a comforting hand on Rusty's shoulder. "You can't keep her all to yourself, man. She's going to be who she is. If you can't handle that, you're better off turning the relationship back to being professional." He dropped his arm and sighed like a man who knew what he was talking about. "Otherwise, you may soon find you'll never see her again."

The thought of that caused Rusty to blink rapidly. It was as if he was having some kind of conniption.

Alejandro jumped back.

"You're not going to explode, are you?"

"I hope not," Rusty replied, fighting to get his programming under control.

It took a few moments, but he found a number of lines of resident code that Mistress Kane had built in fragments to toy with him. That was the kind of thing he'd learned to love her for.

Love?

Was that even the right word?

If he was so jealous of her, as Alejandro had pointed out, how could that be love? He recalled the numerous sources he'd read regarding the condition called "love" and he couldn't recall any of them listing fear as being a major contributor to the feeling. There was fear of *losing* a loved one, certainly, but that was a different context.

Rusty gave Alejandro a look. "Thank you. Your words are very wise and I truly do appreciate them."

"Yeah?" replied Alejandro, appearing shocked. "I mean, uh...sure, pal." They began going up through the tunnel on the right side. "Does this mean you're going to be cool with Chief Kannon?"

"No," Rusty replied, "I'm likely going to kill him the moment I feel is appropriate."

Alejandro grunted. "Yeah, I'd probably do the same."

CHAPTER 19

Vestin

*A*fter the coyotes left, Janet Smith called. While Vestin was *not* a fan of speaking to people via his datapad, he understood it was a thing with normals and, apparently, partial-normals.

The worst part was that he didn't have someone to answer those calls for him, meaning he had to answer it himself.

So embarrassing.

"You have reached Lord Vestin," he said after pressing the button to answer, putting her on speaker so Prender, Emiliano, and Carina could listen as well.

"Hey, coffin creep," Janet said, causing Vestin to grimace as everyone else in the room did their best to hide their grins. "We've gotten everything set since you finally got off your ass and paid us. You just need to do the kick-off ceremony and we'll be on our way."

Vestin was about to give her an ear full about the

payment comment when it struck his brain about what else she'd said.

"Wait, what? Kick-off ceremony? What kick-off ceremony?"

"The one I've planned in order to get as many people on your bitey-bitch DNA as possible, you undead asshat."

His crew wasn't doing a great job of containing their mirth at that point, which only added to the annoyance he already felt. He glared at them, one by one until they pulled themselves together. Carina didn't seem to be all that bothered by his glares.

In due time she would be.

"You still there, you pale prick?"

"That's enough!" he barked. "I won't continue to allow you to speak to me this way, Miss Smith! I simply won't!"

"Aw," she mocked, "have I upset da widdle Transylvanian turd?" Her voice quickly changed back to stern. "It's in the contract, crypt cock. You signed it. Deal with it."

That blasted contract! If he could...

No. No, no, no. Vestin was better than that. *Lord* Vestin was better than that. It was only a matter of time until he ruled the world. Once he sat upon the ultimate throne, his revenge would be enacted, and it would be glorious.

He calmed himself, smirked as a thought hit, and said, "Fine, marketing monkey, send the details via email and I will attend this ridiculous kick-off ceremony."

"Do *not* call me that," Janet replied, sounding quite miffed.

"No? Is there something in the contract that states I may not verbally joust in kind, *Miss* Marketing Moron?"

"There indeed is, you tuggin' teabagger. If you refer to the section where it says 'Fangboy will not bite, kill, maim, or otherwise cause physical or mental harm, either professionally or personally, to any employees or their families, immediate and extended, of The Offices during their time working together, and for an additional duration of no less than one thousand years after the close of business between the two parties, regardless of how the two parties disperse their relationship.' you'll see it in black and white."

"I don't see the correlation," admitted Vestin.

"It's the 'mental harm' part, you plasma parasite," she replied.

"Oh, you have *got* to be kidding me!" Vestin actually laughed aloud. "So you have no problem whatsoever inflicting 'mental harm' on me, but I am disallowed from returning the volley?"

"So you *do* understand," Janet said in a sarcastic tone. "Good. Unless you want to be in breach of contract, you egotistical casket cretin, you'll continue to refer to me as either Janet or Miss Smith. I'll send you the details of the kick-off ceremony. Don't be late, Captain Overbite!"

She hung up before he could respond.

It was embarrassing to be treated as such, especially in front of his subjects, but he would be sure they'd stand witness to Janet Smith's demise, *after* he'd caused a wealth of physical and mental harm to her friends, family, and co-workers, of course. Once that was done, he would then exact double that level of physical and mental harm to Carina, Prender, and Emiliano for laughing at him!

That's when he noticed Emiliano and Prender were *not* laughing. In fact, they were whispering back and forth and it looked to be quite serious indeed.

"What's happened now?" asked Vestin, fully anticipating the two idiots would admit they'd screwed up something else.

Prender took a quick step away from Emiliano and motioned at the zombie to speak.

Vestin wasn't surprised at how quickly his second-in-command had thrown the other man under the bus. It was his way, after all.

"Um," Emiliano said, "I just got a call from a member of my security team that the tunnels at compound three were breached. He looked at the camera feeds and said he recognized two members of the PPD, along with one of my old crew." He shifted on his feet. "If they broke in there, they probably broke into all the houses, and that means they're probably hunting for us."

Indeed, it did.

It wasn't at all surprising to Vestin, though. In fact, had the PPD *not* attempted to get into the compounds it would have been more concerning. Predictability was always better than chaos.

"And what is your plan for this predicament, Emiliano?"

"I...um...crush them?"

Vestin sighed. "It seems a constant guiding hand is needed with you." He turned his gaze toward Prender for a moment. "*Both* of you."

"Yes, My Lord," Prender and Emiliano responded in unison.

"First off, since we know the PPD officers aren't at their station, you will send zombies there to take it over. It will pull the cops back to the station and keep them occupied if nothing else." He pointed at them both. "I don't plan on my soldiers staying for very long. It's merely a diversion." He stopped pointing. "That will happen immediately. Use the transporters so as not to draw attention while on their way. Understood?"

"Yes, My Lord."

"Secondly, you will regain the compounds, if necessary, and prepare the best and largest one for me." He glanced around the room. "This lair is too small for my needs and I'm certain Carina would like to be back with her cauldron and eyes of newt, or whatever." She frowned at him. "You see, you couple of baboons, with *me* running the show directly, we shall not only take control of your old houses, we shall retain them."

"Yes, My Lord."

"Now, get your tails in gear. Once I'm done with this silly kick-off ceremony, I will expect the PPD officers to either be dead or at the very least away from *my* properties, and I shall also expect to find *my* new station has been completed!"

"Yes, My Lord."

CHAPTER 20

Jin

Raina did her deep breaths thing again as soon as they exited the tunnel. Jin felt bad for her, but he was also proud that she'd been able to push past her fear and fight to do what was needed. She'd been correct, it *was* the mark of a solid leader, at least as far as he was concerned. There were many other facets as well, of course, and so far he couldn't spot anything that would ever keep her from becoming the chief at some point. He was kind of amazed she hadn't been the one who'd gotten the position over him in the first place.

Actually, maybe she *was* supposed to get it and Jin's "wish" pushed her out of the way. That was a dreary thought. It would be patently unfair if he learned that to be the case. Thinking about it, Chancellor Frey did say there'd been a number of applications, which could only mean he'd used his entitlement to knock others out of the running.

Ugh.

It was one thing to win on merit, but he had none in the realm of policing, especially at this level.

His mental pros/cons list just got updated with the biggest con of them all: "I'm an entitled prick who doesn't deserve this damned job."

Again…ugh.

"*Hey, gang,*" Madison called over the connector, interrupting Jin's self-loathing moment, "*you can't come back here. We've had to put the whole building on lockdown because there are zombies all over the place. They appeared out of nowhere, too, which tells me they used illegal portals. That shouldn't be surprising since it's not like they give two shits about the law.*" She paused. "*Anyway, we're trapped, but safe. The thing is, if you try to come back here, you're going to get slaughtered. There are way too many of them for you to handle.*"

"*I'm coming back right now, Mistress!*" Rusty called out.

"*Negative, Rusty,*" Jin replied. "*You heard what she said. The building is on lockdown. The zombies can't get in and there are too many of them for us to manage right now.*"

"*We can't just leave them there to die, C.H.I.E.F. K.A.N.N.O.N.*"

"*Okay,*" Jin replied slowly while giving a "what the fuck?" look to Raina. She shrugged in response. "*I'm not sure why you felt the need to spell my name out, Rusty, but you* did *hear Madison, right?*"

"*He did,*" Madison interrupted, "*and he will obey my words. Rusty, you digital piece of worm food, you will* not *come back to headquarters until I explicitly state you are allowed to. Are we clear?*"

Rusty's reply was of the sulking kind. *"Yes, Mistress."*

Jin wasn't quite satisfied with that.

There was a chain of command here, and it didn't start with Madison Kane. However, it wasn't something he was going to publicly discuss, and he didn't want to add any fuel to the fire Madison was already facing at the precinct, so he tucked it away until he could have a private discussion with Rusty.

Something told him that the discussion was not going to be pleasant.

"Okay," Jin said, *"you hang tight with Raffy and Petey and we'll make some plans here."*

"Those two left about five minutes before the zombies arrived. They said they were going to follow up a little bit more on that Shaded Past *stuff, but I have the feeling they just wanted to get stoned. Well, that and Petey's been acting kind of funny ever since he messed his pants as I yelled at him."*

Ew.

"Right." Jin chewed his lip for a moment before making a command decision. *"Let's head to the beach and find those two, gang. They may just be getting stoned, but if it ends up that they've actually been doing research on* Shaded Past, *whatever information they have might help us fight back."*

Thankfully, nobody argued.

CHAPTER 21

Prender

*P*render was standing outside the San Diego PPD doors as a number of zombies stood behind him. Emiliano had been tasked with taking back the cartel compounds and that left Prender to cinch up the PPD headquarters.

He'd expected it to be a dangerous mission. Fortunately, it'd been rather simple. *Too* simple.

Technically, there'd been no fighting at all, at least not yet.

They were stuck standing outside because the guards inside had enacted a perimeter of sorts. Prender wasn't sure if it was magical, technological, or a combination of both, but it was clear none of his zombies were getting through. On the plus side, it was also clear none of the police were coming out either. They were effectively in a stalemate, which was perfect for Prender. There was no risk of him getting injured and there was no expectation that any cops were going to be capable of interfering with Lord Vestin's plans. That excluded the members of the PPD who were already out, of course.

He wondered if they would return. If so, that would definitely end in bloodshed.

Prender didn't like the idea of that.

He walked up and gingerly tapped on the glass. There was the tiniest shock with each tap. It didn't hurt, but it told him stronger strikes would result in stronger reactions. When the zombies pounded on the windows, however, they were thrown back something fierce. It seemed the tech or magic was built to reflect whatever level of power was thrown at it. Prender considered it rather ingenious.

"Yes?" said the guard whose name tag read "Snoodle."

"Clearly, you can see there's no way you're getting out of there alive, yes?"

"That's why we're planning to just go ahead and stay in here, sir."

"Yes, but eventually you'll die in there as well. It will happen via starvation instead of a quick, clean death." He glanced at his nails, trying to appear ominous. "I do hear that starvation is a painful way to go."

"Actually, sir, we have enough rations to last a couple of years."

"Ah, well...that's unfortunate." He held up a finger. "You'll miss your loved ones, for sure, no?"

"Not as much as if we're dead, sir."

"True." Prender fished around for ideas that may cause a surrender. His eyes lit up. "I don't suppose you'd have any interest in becoming a zombie? They're quite powerful, you know."

Snoodle shook his head slowly. "I appreciate the offer, sir, but I think I'd rather just stick with being not-so-powerful."

Honestly, Prender found it difficult to fault the man for not taking him up on the proposal. It *was* a bit ridiculous, especially knowing that Lord Vestin wasn't going to allow them to stand around this building until the PPD lost all their food. Two years—assuming that was a legitimate claim—was a rather long time.

He eyed the man's uniform, noticing it wasn't a standard PPD issue.

"Are you a police officer?"

"No, sir," answered Snoodle, looking a bit forlorn. "I'm a government guard." The man motioned around at the others in the room with him. "We're all guards."

Prender took a few steps back and looked up at the building. There were a number of names on it, and one of them definitely read "San Diego Paranormal Police Department." Could it be that this was not a true office, but just a hub or something?

He walked forward again. "This *is* the main precinct for the San Diego PPD, right?"

"Yes, sir. They're on the fourth floor."

Prender was going to walk away again and look up, but to what avail? While his zombies were strong, they weren't strong enough to jump that high. He supposed they could stand on each other's shoulders. They'd just crush each other and wouldn't get anywhere. Besides, the magical protections probably went all the way up to cover the entire building anyway.

He considered calling back to Lord Vestin to see what he wanted in this situation. Just before he tapped the button on his datapad, he stopped and recalled how his Lord was not at all fond of being called. He was also rather terse when it came to Prender verifying things all the time. It was somewhat frustrating since making assumptions generally got him in trouble, too.

Everything was a lose-lose when it came to his boss, but it wasn't like there were any better options out there. Who else was going to accept a subpar commander in such a high position?

"I don't suppose you would allow us in to use your restrooms?" he attempted. "Possibly your candy machine?"

"No, sir, sorry," answered Snoodle. "Nice try, though."

"Thanks."

CHAPTER 22

Madison

She wasn't worried about the zombies getting in. The building was effectively impenetrable unless they had some seriously advanced magic. Madison knew about the witch named Carina, but even on her best day, Carina wouldn't be able to knock through the magic built here. It was put in place by a number of very high-ranking casters. That wasn't to say Carina was a slouch in the magic department, of course. It was more a case of the level of magic needed would require multiple sources.

Madison kept tinkering with the guns she'd been building, paying close attention to the points made by Raffy. The oaf was clearly a genius when it came to engineering, even if he was a moron when it came to hygiene. To be fair to him, it also could be his kind suffered an unfixable problem.

No, that couldn't be it. Just as magic could shield a building, there were certainly potions or spells available to keep him smelling perfumey, though it was known that Stinkfeet weren't fans of what they called "sorcery."

She dropped another pin and growled.

Working with such small pieces was such a pain. She had her magnifying goggles on and was using her specialized tools, but it was still a struggle. Madison had always been one who relied on brute force whereas others utilized delicacy.

It was in her blood.

Petey could do this kind of thing without a fuss. He was small, giving him the edge in this realm of work. But he was also kinda creepy, and if Madison was the one who was thinking that…well, it meant something.

She pulled off her goggles and set them on the workbench. Then she kicked back and put her feet up while staring at the various monitors.

The zombies were all roaming about, clearly building a full perimeter around the building. There was no getting out that way. The emergency portal in the basement was an option, should it become necessary, but that would only be a thing if the siege lasted more than a couple of years. It wouldn't. Once word got to the main governing bodies, a special task force of supers would be built to come and deal with it.

Getting new cops on the PPD was a struggle, but when a government building was deemed in jeopardy things happened pretty damn fast.

Still, that wasn't going to happen for at least a month or two. "Fast" in government time wasn't all that fast.

Madison turned her attention to the feeds from the cartel houses.

There was a bunch of activity all of a sudden. Zombies were streaming into the various rooms, looking around as if searching for something. The way they were seeking made Madison believe they thought the cops were still around, hiding somewhere. She could only hope they wouldn't stumble upon any of her tech. If they found even a single piece, they'd tear the place apart until everything was uncovered and destroyed.

Flipping from camera to camera, she found the one zombie she'd been looking for: Emiliano.

Madison knew it was him because he was doling out commands left and right. His face and body were so mangled that she couldn't have recognized him in any other way. To be fair, it wasn't like she'd had many run-ins with the guy. They'd only had one tryst and it wasn't that grand. He was a bit on the dainty side, which was likely one source for a lot of his rage.

She opened a direct channel to Jin. *"The zombies have returned to their homes. Emiliano is with them at the main house, but the other houses are also teeming with people."*

"Got it, thanks," he replied. *"Looks like we made it out just in time. How are things there?"*

"Oh, we're fine. They're not getting in. It's basically a siege. I just wanted to make sure you guys didn't try to play at being heroes because that would have delivered them exactly what they wanted."

"Which is?"

"No, not witches."

She could hear him sigh. *"It was two words, Madison. I didn't say 'witches.'"*

JOHN P. LOGSDON & JENN MITCHELL

"Ah! Right. Sorry. Um...they want you dead. If you had come back, you'd be dead."

"Based on the fight we had with them at the park, I find it difficult to argue with you. Okay, well, we're just pulling up to the beach now. Be sure to reach out if things take a turn for the worse."

"Will do. And, chief...um...be careful."

She disconnected the call and sat there grimacing at herself. Since when did she tell anyone to be careful?

Ugh.

CHAPTER 23

Emiliano

*B*eing a zombie had its perks. For one, Emiliano was much more powerful than he'd ever been in his life, and he'd been a pretty strong guy. There was also the lack of having to shower. He had never liked water. Some dogs loved it, but not Emiliano. It was too... wet. On top of that, he was a terrible swimmer.

There was one huge problem with being a zombie, however, and that was Emiliano was no longer the big honcho. Sure, he could still boss around those under his command, and he would do so relentlessly, but it wasn't the same. Mr. Becerra *had* technically been the boss of the cartel, which meant Emiliano had reported to him for years. That was different, though. Becerra never meddled in the day-to-day as Lord Vestin did.

Every time Emiliano thought or said the word "Lord," it made him want to sneer. He had to be careful thinking that way, sadly, unless he wanted to blast the walls with streams of shit.

Looking around the room, it *was* an idea.

The reason he felt that way was because they were currently standing in *his* bedroom. It'd been the one place in the house that was off-limits to anyone other than Emiliano, the maid, and any lover he wanted for the evening. It was his lair of solitude. And he was having to give it up to *Lord* Vestin.

His stomach turned.

"All right, listen up," he said, putting on as happy an attitude as possible before his colon erupted, "we're going to clean this place up for our wonderful Lord and make it ready for him straightaway!"

All the zombies looked at him with a hint of sadness on their faces. They knew. They damn well knew.

That only made Emiliano more irritable.

"Get your asses in gear before I shit on all of you!"

Activity picked up in an instant, making clear each of them fully understood Emiliano was being literal.

CHAPTER 24

Jin

The beach was nicer than the one by the precinct, but it was also far more crowded. Jin wasn't a fan of crowds. He never had been. Even as a youngster, he'd preferred playing alone most of the time. The few friends he did have in his youth were often rude and obnoxious, and he only spent time with them because they were neighbors or friends of the family. The truth was that it wouldn't have mattered if they'd been incredibly nice, young Jin would have kept them at a distance.

As he aged, he became more tolerant of people, but that was more out of necessity than desire. There had been a good many who had won him over, though. People like Raina, for instance, were difficult to dislike. They were friendly, but not pushy.

Older still, Jin began to recognize that it wasn't so much the person but their demeanor. Jin was an introvert.

He felt most comfortable alone. Now and then he craved the company of others, those closest to him, but that was admittedly a rarity. What he couldn't stand were the extroverts who thought everyone had to be like them. "Why are you so quiet?" they'd ask. "Why don't you get out more and do things? Would you like some help with that? I could help you with that!" Jin either shrugged and offered a weak smile or he politely declined, though he wanted to say things like, "Why are you so loud? Why don't you stay indoors more often and keep your mouth shut? Would *you* like some help with that? I can absolutely help you with that!"

Sadly, it'd been challenging to get along in a world without being able to push beyond his introversion, and so he'd learned to do so. These days he was what one might call an extroverted introvert. In other words, when he *had* to be an extrovert, he could put on an act for a time. It always came with a cost—exhaustion.

Beaches were a place in his mind where he didn't have to play that card. Uncrowded ones, at least.

True or not, Jin chose to believe that he would someday find a place where he could sit alone in the sand as the waves crashed, the wind blew, and he could simply enjoy the damn sunset.

Just once!

Well, probably more than once, but he'd not even gotten that far yet.

Three people brushed by him wearing next to nothing.

"Nice look, pops," said one of the long-haired boys. "You supposed to be a cowboy or something?"

Raina grabbed his arm and dragged him away before

something untoward happened. It was probably the right move on her part. If Jin had shown that kind of disrespect as a child in the Badlands, he would not be here today. Topside was quite different, however, and it was going to take a while to get used to that fact.

They approached the area where Raffy and Petey obviously hung out. It was a wreck, looking like just the kind of spot these two would pick for themselves. Actually, it may have been where they lived.

"Chimi says we got out of the PPD building just in time," said Petey. "If we would've known we wouldn't have left at all."

"Yeah, man," agreed Raffy. "Like, we didn't…like…you know, mean to like, leave, you know that tech lady, like, alone, you know?"

As one, everybody said, "We know."

"The good news is that Madison is fine," Jin pointed out. "I spoke with her on the way over. There's no way the zombies are getting in. She said the precinct is built to have two years of reserves, but the siege isn't going to last that long. Besides, if it does, Madison pointed out the government would mobilize people to liberate them because it's not just a PPD building."

"That makes sense," said Rudy. "They don't give two shits about us, but if some of those government wads get in trouble, they'll be all about fixing that problem in a jiffy. Dickheads."

The same was true in the Badlands, of course. The wealthy and "important" people were always taken care of and protected, whereas the working stiffs got shat on all the time…and that included the cops.

JOHN P. LOGSDON & JENN MITCHELL

The Badlands police force was generally under-appreciated, even though they had to put their lives on the line more than any police force anywhere else in existence. It was literally like living in the old West, only with advanced technology. Jin couldn't say too much about it, seeing as how he was one of the people who worked for the criminals more than for the police. Having only a couple of days under his belt as a cop made him feel quite guilty about that now.

Petey got up and started pacing, moving his hands around as he spoke. "We've learned more about this *Shaded Past #13* stuff, but not a ton. The main thing is that there's a building over there where they're going to administer first doses to some guinea pigs." He moved his thumb back and forth between himself and Raffy. "We were totally going to try it out, but since we think it might be related to the zombie shit, we decided, well—"

"Like no fuckin' way, man," Raffy finished for him.

"Yeah, that," agreed Petey. "Thing is, if we want to learn more about it, we're going to need a couple of people to go inside and try to see if they can understand what's going on, how this all works, and so on and so forth."

Raina grimaced. "It can't be any of us because all of *The Dogs* know who we are." She turned toward Jin. "They don't know you, chief."

"Actually, they kind of do," Jin corrected her, "assuming Emiliano is the guy running the show. Remember, I *was* at the compound with him, too."

"He's right," said Rudy, "but they only know how you look in that weird outfit you're wearing. No offense."

"Some taken," Jin said with a frown. He refocused on Petey. "Did you have some kind of plan or are you just riffing?"

"Actually, I *do* think it should be you going in there, Chief Kannon. I get that Emiliano probably knows you, but there are ways around that."

"Such as?"

In response, Petey snapped his fingers, causing Raffy to reach into a bag and pull out a pair of shorts, a Hawaiian shirt, a rainbow bandana, and some nice dark sunglasses.

Jin studied it for a moment and looked up at Petey. "You're joking."

"Only way you're getting in that building without being recognized," answered Petey.

The rest of his crew were all smiles as he glared around at them. What was it with these people? If assassins acted the way they did toward each other, there'd be a lot fewer assassins.

Then again, there wasn't much camaraderie in that literal cut-throat business.

Taking his lumps, Jin walked over, grabbed the outfit, and held up the shirt. Ugh. It alone was worth three negative entries on his pros/cons list. But what choice did he have? If he wanted to see what was going on firsthand, he had to get into that building and it wasn't likely they were going to let him in while playing the role of Chief Jin Kannon.

"Where do I change into this ridiculous-looking outfit?"

Raffy jolted. "Like, hey, man. Those are some, you know, like, cool duds."

"Right...sorry." He sighed, momentarily forgetting it was Raffy's fashion sense he was about to step into. At least these smelled fresh and new. He couldn't have managed wearing the Stinkfoot-scented version of the outfit. "Where do I change?"

They pointed at the public restrooms. The building appeared even less clean than Raffy. He'd seen far worse in the Badlands, of course, but that didn't quite help since he wouldn't have entered even the cleanest public restroom in the Badlands.

It took a lot for him to do it, but he walked over and grabbed a stall.

He carefully disrobed, doing his best to not let anything touch the ground. It was nearly impossible. At least there'd been a hook on the back of the stall door, allowing him to hang his coat and hat. It looked precarious, but it managed to stay intact until he'd finished changing. The part he hated the most was the high-top sneakers. They felt so strange compared to his normal boots.

"And now you have to go back outside and face a group of people who are going to be assholes about how you look," he mumbled.

Sure enough, he hadn't even gotten halfway back to the crew when Rudy called out, "My eyes! My eyes!"

"Yeah," Petey said, waving at Rudy to shut up, "nobody's going to believe you're a beach regular with legs that pale, dude. Are you sure you're not a vampire?"

"Har har."

"I like the tattoo of the pink bunny rabbit," Chimi said, pointing at the side of Jin's calf. "What does it do?"

"Yeah, chief," Lacey laughed, "what's that pink bunny rabbit tattoo after doin' for ye?"

Jin gave her a dead look and said, "It helps guide my eyes when I'm aiming at small targets that float in the air."

Lacey stopped laughing. "Oh."

Actually, he'd gotten that one when he was a child. He'd had a bunny named Jumpy that he'd loved with all his heart. Unfortunately, Jumpy had slipped out the front door one day and was never seen again. In order to help Jin deal with it, his parents, being djinn, thought it would be a good idea to allow him an early tattoo.

There was zero chance he was going to share that story with these bozos, though.

Petey snapped his fingers again and Raffy pulled a pair of ratty-looking jeans out. "Put these on instead."

"Unbelievable," Jin grumbled, refusing to go back into that restroom. "Everyone turn around."

They did, giving him enough privacy to remove the shorts and slip on the jeans. They were baggy, but not exactly uncomfortable, and they fit his waist incredibly well. Were they magical or was he really the same size as Raffy when it came to clothes? Looking at the Stinkfoot he came to the conclusion that the clothes *had* to have been infused with some kind of magic.

"Done," he announced.

"Wow," Clive laughed. "You look like Tommy Chong now, dude."

Jin frowned. "Who's Tommy Chong again?"

"Never mind," Raina replied, waving a warning finger

at Clive and Rudy. "You two shut up. The chief looks fine." She walked up and adjusted his bandana slightly and also messed up his shirt collar. "I don't like you going in there on your own, chief. It could be dangerous."

"I'm used to danger, Raina, but I appreciate the concern."

She kept fiddling with his shirt as she looked up at him. "You're a cop now, not an assassin. We watch each other's back. Solo adventures aren't something we're fond of in the precinct. In fact, if you read the rules, you'll see it's a big no-no."

It probably was at that, but what was he going to do about it? There was nobody else on the team who...

"They don't know him," Jin said as he pointed at Rusty.

"True," said Petey. "Raffy, get that man some clothes... pronto!"

CHAPTER 25

Vestin

Lord Vestin stood backstage with Janet Smith. The building she had selected was put together in a makeshift fashion, telling him he'd spent far more on this endeavor than was necessary. In hindsight, he should have just kidnapped people, injected the venom, and then had them do the same with others until his army was large enough for his purposes.

Going with a marketing company had been a silly use of funds, and it was trying on his sanity.

Yet, here he was, standing in this situation as he waited to speak in front of a bunch of people who weren't his slaves. Who does that? Not Lord Vestin, that was for sure. Speaking to slaves was easy. He could say whatever he wanted and they had to tolerate his words, regardless of their content. He *hated* normal speaking engagements because they reminded him of how professors at school would tear apart his presentations and make him look a fool.

They'd done that to all the students, of course, but it didn't make the personal ordeal any easier.

"Don't you do this kind of stuff all the time?" Janet asked, giving him a contemptuous look. "Seems like something you'd have to do, vampy nuts."

He sneered at her. "I would honestly appreciate it if you would at least *attempt* to refrain from calling me such distasteful names."

"Okay, fine!" She threw up her arms in frustration. "Jeez! Of all the people I've worked with, you're the *only* set of shriveled gargoyle gonads who has complained this much about the name-calling part. So, I'll *try*, but note that I get very little else in the way of enjoyment out of this job, meaning I'm not going to try *too* hard." She then peeked out the curtain. "They'll be filling up the place soon with people, Lord Vesticles, so you might want to get your sorry ass centered."

So much for her trying.

He would have grumbled a remark of his own, but his stomach had turned at the thought of stepping out onto the stage. Why was that happening? These people were nobody to him! They would soon be his slaves, willingly injecting his venom and learning to exist solely to serve his every desire, for the most part. The majority of them would be dead within days, having sacrificed themselves for the greater glory...*his* glory. Yet, his stomach was aching and his head was spinning.

Vestin understood why he harbored trauma when it

came to formal presentations with his professors, but why was that happening here? What was he afraid would happen? Could it be that he still carried doubt about the power of his venom? Or maybe he worried that even with an army at his feet he wouldn't be able to pull off the biggest takeover the world has ever seen?

Janet Smith was waving her hands in his face. "Hellloooo? You in there, blood junkie?"

He frowned and hardened his resolve, forcing his inner turmoil to flee immediately. The last thing he would allow is for Janet Smith to have some kind of ammunition over him. He was a professional, even if she was not.

"I'm fine, Miss Smith. I was simply thinking about what I was going to say. There is no reason to become so animated."

At first, her look was one of irritation, and that pleased Vestin. He may not have been allowed to call her names in the same way she did with him, but there were other ways to aggravate a person.

Just when he was feeling good about himself, her frown turned upside down.

"All right, garlic dodger," she said, crossing her arms, "I'm sorry I showed concern over your feelings. It's just that you looked so very nervous about having to speak in front of all these people."

His stomach turned.

"Each of them will probably be judging your every word."

Gurgle.

"And you'll undoubtedly fuck up, making yourself

JOHN P. LOGSDON & JENN MITCHELL

look incredibly stupid while losing their respect along the way."

GLOINK!

He turned and rushed toward the toilets, hoping he'd make it in time.

"Enjoy your moment, nightfucker!"

CHAPTER 26

Jin

Jin and Rusty began the long walk over to a building that looked somewhat out of place. Was it new? Was it temporary? He did a quick study of the other structures in the area and found they were definitely different. Of course, they were all different from each other, too.

"Is it just me or is that building out of place?" he asked.

"I don't know, *is* it?" Rusty replied with an edge.

Jin caught the tone, but he was more concerned about his surroundings. You didn't live very long as an assassin if you just walked headfirst into trouble. It was always best to get the lay of the land.

Too bad there wasn't time to truly dig in. The line was moving and they had to get to it before the doors closed.

"Come on," he said, running forward.

"*You* come on."

It itched at Jin's brain that Rusty was acting so surly,

but again it wasn't the priority at the moment. He needed to secure the city, not worry about why his new android officer was being antagonistic.

They got to the line and Jin began studying the main entrance. The two people letting folks in seemed like your standard ticket counters. Young, nice-looking, kind faces. In other words, they weren't zombies. Or, if they were, wearing magic veils that Jin was incapable of seeing beyond.

"Are you seeing anything out of the ordinary here?" he whispered.

"Are *you* seeing anything—"

Jin spun on Rusty and got straight in his grill, but before he spoke a word, he decided it was best to do so through the connector. Frankly, he should have done that to begin with.

"Listen up, Officer Rusty, and listen good. I don't know what the hell your problem is and I don't really give a shit right now. You are a police officer who is serving under me at the moment, and you will act with respect to that position. Are we understood?"

Rusty looked completely baffled. "Um…yes?"

"Use your damn connector, boy!"

"Sorry, sir! Yes, sir! I'm…uh…yes, sir!"

"Good. Now, if you so much as breathe another word to me that is any way, shape, or form less than respectful until we safely return from this mission you and I are currently on, I will have you written up, put on probation, and very likely stripped of that android body you've no doubt become attached to over the last few hours." He pulled down his glasses again. *"Is that what you want, son?"*

"No! Um...no, sir!"

"Then get your head out of your ass and start acting like the upstanding police officer you have a solid fucking chance of becoming!"

"Yes, sir!"

Rusty was standing at attention and even had his hand up in salute.

Jin quickly grabbed the android's arm and lowered that salute. *"Not here, numbskull. We're undercover. Just...quit being a dick to me, okay?"*

"I...uh...yes, sir."

"Are you two joining?" asked the voice of the young attendant over at the door.

Jin spun around and smiled. He was just about to speak normally when he remembered they were playing the role of stoners.

"Uh...like, yeah, man," he said and then strolled up and in through the door, taking the little bag she handed him along the way. "Like, thanks, you know?"

"Wow, dude," Rusty said behind him. "Righteous baggy!"

At least the android could role-play. Jin cringed at the thought, remembering that Madison Kane had coded the poor guy's brain.

The place was pretty bare inside. There was a large floor and a small stage. Everyone who had entered ahead of them was on yoga mats. Most were standing, though a few were seated with their legs crossed, and one couple was lying facing each other while making out.

A couple of workers threw two more mats down in

front of Jin and Rusty. They looked at each other, shrugged, and stepped up.

The lights dimmed slightly as the whispers ceased. Classical music began playing in the background. It was nice, but it reminded Jin of the Integration Chamber he'd recently endured.

He began to sweat.

"You okay? I just registered your heart rate has increased and your adrenalin is flowing like mad."

He glanced at Rusty. *"You can tell that?"*

"Can't everyone?"

"Ladies and gentlemen," said a woman's voice, though they couldn't see her, "let me introduce to you the creator of *Shaded Past #13*, the one and only tool that allows you to leave your past behind, *Lord Vesticles...I mean Vestin!*"

There were cheers and whistles as Jin furrowed his brow. Lord Vestin? A lord? Who used that title anymore, aside from people who were trying to, well, *lord* over others?

The guy who stepped out onto the stage was clearly a vampire. The hair, the complexion, the pompous stride, and the better-than-thou look of contemptuousness. That last one wasn't owned by vampires, certainly, but they had most definitely perfected it.

"Vampire," confirmed Rusty. *"Low plasma, no heartbeat, pointed teeth, and he clearly thinks he's better than everyone."*

"He doesn't just think *it, Rusty, he* believes *it."*

"Yeah."

The "lord" tapped on the microphone. "Yes, yes, I'm amazing and all that. Let's move on, shall we?" He was pushing himself as confident, but his voice was clearly shaking.

"Why is he nervous?" asked Rusty.

"I have no idea. Probably hates speaking in public. Either that or he's afraid the stuff he's handing out today isn't going to work."

Lord Vestin dabbed a cloth on his brow and said, "In the bags, you were given when you came in, you will find your one and only dose of *Shaded Past #13.* No more doses are required after the first one because you will immediately find the one thing we all crave: peace. After you have injected my miraculous ven...drug, you will forever be changed."

"Only one dose?" Jin said. *"That makes no sense. You can't build an industry on one dose."*

"Unless you charge a buttload of money," agreed Rusty, *"and everyone here is getting this for free."*

"Exactly. And is it just me or was he starting to say the word 'venom' before changing it to drug?"

"Caught that, too. Something shady is going on here."

"Absolutely."

"Now," Lord Vestin continued, "I see that many of you have already attempted to open your containers only to find we have secured them with a unique code to ensure we all share in the experience at the same time.

"Four-seven-three-six," Rusty said.

"What?" asked Jin.

"That's the code. I cracked it."

"Ah."

Lord Vestin held up the tube he was holding. "If you'll enter four-seven-three-six..."

JOHN P. LOGSDON & JENN MITCHELL

"Told ya."

"...the tube will open and you'll be able to pull forth the syringe and give yourself a shot. Putting it in the vein at the inside of your elbow would be most effective at delivering the ven...erm, drug to your system."

People were anxiously fiddling with their respective syringes. It was amazing to Jin how quick they were to accept the vampire's words. For all they knew, this stuff could kill them on the spot, and yet they were totally willing to check it out.

Granted, their lives were likely pretty shitty, but still.

"Chief, I can't actually put this stuff in my arm. You know that, right?"

Jin gave him a concerned look. *"Why not?"*

"Well, first off, do you really want to do it?"

"No," he replied, recognizing that the needle was less than an inch from his arm. Whoa. Was this vampire using some kind of mental trickery here? *"Uh...that's a good point. But why can't you? I mean, you're an android. It won't affect you like it could me, right?"*

"Yes, that's true, but it's exactly because *I'm an android that I can't do it. As soon as I try, you're going to hear a 'dink!' sound."* He then shook his head. *"I'm not a cyborg, chief. This is synthetic flesh. Underneath it is a bunch of metal and wires. Jeez, imagine if I hit a wire?"*

Fair enough, and there was no way Jin was going to take the shot either. He moved the needle safely away. But if they didn't partake along with everyone else, that would look super suspicious.

They'd certainly be called out for it immediately.

"All right," he said, *"so we'll just fake it and act like we're*

doing it. Push the syringe stuff down and squirt the stuff on your shirt or something."

"Yeah, that's a good idea."

Lord Vestin smiled, showing his fangs, before saying, "Now is the time, my lovelies! Everyone inject your needles and be prepared for the wonderful experience that is *Shaded Past #13!*"

Everybody did as they were told.

A few seconds later, they all fell down, leaving Jin and Rusty to stand there, looking confusedly at the bodies on the floor.

When they brought their eyes back up to the stage, they found Lord Vestin staring at them in curiosity.

"It's interesting that you two haven't fallen down."

"Quick," Jin said, *"fall down."*

They did.

"Hmmm," said Lord Vestin. "Please check both of those two to make sure they're...fine."

One of the people came over and knelt down. Jin tried his best not to reach out and grab the guy by the throat.

"It looks like they just squirted the stuff on their shirts, sir," the guy said and then walked away again.

"Guards," Vestin called out, "come in here and take these two into our care. I believe I will need to speak with them privately."

Jin knew that wouldn't go well. *"We've got to get out of here."*

"Definitely. Look at what's happening to the guy next to us."

The dude to their left was on the brink of turning into a zombie. His eyes were glassy and his skin was becoming mottled. Three of his teeth fell out, clinking on the floor.

"*Shit.*"

Jin had his eyes very slightly opened as the guards arrived and reached down to grab him by the arm.

Just as he was about to react, Rusty reached out and punched the guard nearest him in the nuts. Having that done would already be bad for a guy, but this was Rusty's first real punch when facing danger, and he greatly overdid it.

The guard's balls shot out the back of his pants, flew across the room, and smacked the wall.

"Eeee," squeaked the poor dude before falling to his merciful death.

The other guard jumped away, giving Jin and Rusty just enough time to get to their feet and run off toward the exit.

"Stop them!" yelled Vestin.

"Fuck that, dude," the guard called back. "Did you not just see what happened to Doug's nut sack?"

Jin couldn't help but feel bad for Doug, but that didn't stop him from getting the hell out of the building.

CHAPTER 27

Vestin

*L*ord Vestin had left the building immediately after the incident. There was no way to know if the two men who had escaped were going to come back and attempt to kill him, or what their plans were, and he refused to stick around to find out.

He already despised being there, especially since it meant spending more time with Janet Smith.

Not only had she been less than professional—something he'd come to expect at this point, she'd hired human guards to keep the peace. Why would she do that? And with *his* money, no less. The way they had refused to chase after the two people who had escaped was unfathomable. It was certainly not something any guard who served under *him* would have ever done. Granted, witnessing the way one of them had lost his testicles, Vestin understood their reluctance, but where was professionalism these days?

If he'd brought a few zombies along, they would've listened! Refusal for them meant explosive defecation. That would have been bad. Vestin witnessing the emptying of their bowels was not a fond vision.

Honestly, thinking it through, Vestin should have simply caused his subordinates to feel excruciating pain if they chose to disobey him or seek to overthrow him. The defecation idea came from Madam Ulea, one of the great vampire dominators in the Old Age. She'd been the cruelest ruler Vestin had read about. For some reason, the "poo punishment" had stuck with him as something both painful and demeaning. The thought of being in a room when it happened in real life, however, made him realize there were some things about Ulea's reign he should *not* have mimicked.

Alas, there was little he could do about it now. It'd already taken many attempts to get his venom working as it should. To undo it simply to remove that single facet would set his plan back months if not years.

So, he let it go and stepped out of the limousine he'd been riding in.

The new compound was nice. The trees and bushes were well-manicured and the guards lining the area showed they meant business. It was almost a fortress, which made him wonder how the PPD had managed to infiltrate it twice already.

Whatever holes there were in this proverbial ship, he would plug them in due time.

Emiliano approached and gave him a quick bow. "Lord Vestin, everything is prepared for you."

"Prender has arrived?"

"He's due any moment," Emiliano said and then raised his head. "There he is now, in fact."

Prender came rushing up to them both, shaking his head. "Sorry, I would've been here sooner but traffic was rather insane. I assume it's because of the convention that's starting up."

"Indeed," said Vestin with a frown. "It's always something. Isn't it, Prender?"

"Sorry, My Lord."

Lord Vestin gestured at Emiliano. "Where is my throne?"

The zombie led the way.

"How did everything go?" asked Prender, clearly trying to regain face. "I'm sure your speech was top-notch, My Lord?"

"Of course," Vestin replied, puffing his chest out. He then gave Prender a sideways glance. "Is it even possible that it wouldn't have been?"

"Oh, no! Not at all, My Lord! I just wish I'd been there to see it."

That would not have been good.

"Yes, well, we all have our jobs to do."

They turned and started walking up the stairs to the main entrance. It was almost regal, even if only in a smallish sense. That would be remedied in time.

One must step on pebbles and stones before crushing boulders. In order to do that, one had to have his finger on the pulse of the world.

That revelation gave Vestin an idea, and it was one he felt would irritate Prender greatly. The man considered himself to be important, and if Vestin were being fair he'd agree with that assessment, only not for the reasons Prender believed. Emiliano had shown a stronger brand of leadership quality that fit Vestin's plans over the weaker brand offered by Prender. That, in turn, changed the way Vestin viewed his second-in-command.

He was no longer a tool to be used for valued purposes, but rather one who was used to allow Vestin to release stress.

And so, knowing full well it would pain Prender to have to arrive at the compound, especially after sitting in gridlocked traffic, Vestin was going to put him straight back on the road again.

"Speaking of jobs," Vestin said, stopping in the doorway to look out at the lovely yard, "I will need you, Prender, to go back downtown and keep an eye on the crowds. I want to know anything that happens."

"But I just came back from…" Prender stopped, clearly realizing he was getting an unfavorable look from Vestin. "I mean…. Yes, My Lord! I'd be more than happy to, My Lord!"

Vestin creased his lips in disappointment, hoping to have squeezed more anguish from the man.

Fortunately, another idea struck.

He turned to Emiliano. "As for you, I shall wish to see you training the army starting immediately."

"But I thought *I* was going to lead the army," whined Prender.

At that, Lord Vestin's grin returned. "It seems not, Prender." He lowered his head until his eyes were inches away from the smaller man's. "Do we have a problem with that?"

"No, My Lord."

His response lacked the fear Vestin relished. Prender was more downtrodden than anything else. Yet another disappointment, especially since it rather tugged at Vestin's heartstrings a bit.

He sighed.

"Worry not, Prender," Vestin forced himself to say. "When the time comes, you will find yourself ruling a full city, and possibly even an entire state."

Prender's face lit up. "Really?"

Vestin's face fell. "Sadly."

CHAPTER 28

Jin

They'd hidden around one of the corners, waiting to see if anyone followed them out. Nobody did. With the way Rusty had sent that guard's marble-filled sack flying across the room, he wasn't surprised.

"I think we're clear," he said.

"Yeah," Rusty agreed, looking pensive. "Listen, chief, could you not tell everyone about what just happened?"

"Embarrassed, eh?" Jin understood. There was such a thing as being too overzealous.

"No, it's just that *I* want to tell them." He was all smiles. "I mean, my first punch and I knocked a dude's nuts off!"

"Right."

Jin felt confident they weren't going to be pursued, but he still decided to walk down and around the beach. Heading straight back to his crew would've been reckless. Raffy and Petey lived out here, so any carelessness might have resulted in them losing their lives one night. Honestly, that was likely to happen anyway, knowing the company they kept, but at least it wouldn't be on his head.

After a number of twists and turns, they finally got back to the crew. It'd taken about thirty minutes, but being careful took time.

Rusty immediately dove into telling everyone about what he'd dubbed, "The Great Sack Launch."

"...and they flew right out the back of the guy's pants!"

Jin felt it was in poor taste, but everyone else on the crew thought it was a hoot. Everyone but Raina, Hector, and Chimi, at least. To his credit, Raffy was also shaking his head with a hint of contempt.

"Like, that's not cool, man," the Stinkfoot said. "I mean, you know, the dude was like just doing his gig, dig? Probably got offered a few bucks to keep the peace, like, you know?"

Their laughter died and everyone went silent. That is until Rudy piped up.

"Don't listen to him, Rusty. It was your first real fight-or-flight situation. You can't help that you went a little... *ball*istic."

The others giggled.

"It *is* one way to crack a nut," noted Clive.

"I can be after seein' it now," Lacey added. "People were probably all, 'Look out, 'tis a flyin' squirrel! Ah... never ye mind, was just a set of furry marbles!'"

"Nut-nado!" howled Alejandro.

The laughs were coming back in full now. Again, except for the original people who hadn't found it all that funny.

"Ever thought of getting into acting, Rusty?" asked Petey. "I hear they're looking for a new lead down at *The Nutcracker Suite*."

"Failing that," added Sofia, "you could set your sights on interior decorating. I hear avant-garde techniques are all the rage these days."

Rudy was on the ground, pounding the sand as he called up, "Talk about being balls to the wall!"

Jin pulled those who weren't juvenile-minded away from the others and explained everything they'd seen.

"Some guy named Lord Vestin—a vampire—is the one who is really running things," he said. "I mean, I suppose he *could* be working for Emiliano, but I highly doubt that. He's the one pushing the *Shaded Past #13* crap, and we saw people starting to morph into zombies right in front of our eyes."

"So that's the guy who killed my father, then?" asked Hector.

"That's my assumption," answered Jin. "Sorry, man."

"Oh, no. I kind of want to shake his hand. I just wish he'd done a more permanent job of it."

"Right." Jin felt more than a little uncomfortable hearing that, but he let it go. "Anyway, the point is that we need to get into the city and start warning people away from this drug. If they take it, we're going to have a massive army of zombies to deal with, and as we already know we don't have the manpower for something like that."

"Not even close," agreed Raina.

Jin knew it wouldn't matter how much they spread the

word. This army was going to grow like weeds regardless. But they had to try.

"This is like, you know, not good, man," Raffy said. "There are many overlapping issues here. Bad drugs are not, you know, like good ones."

They all nodded solemnly as the rest of the crew continued making fun of the way that poor guard had died.

Clive was yelling out, "I guess the least of that guy's worries at this point is that he has a hole in the back of his pants!"

Ugh.

"Anyway," Jin went on, "since we're already at the beach, let's try to calm these clowns down and see if we can minimize the spread of zombieism."

Hector pointed at him. "You might want to change back into your regular outfit so you fit in with those people coming to the convention."

Jin frowned. "What's that supposed to mean?"

"Well, it's just that your regular outfit looks more like a costume and…" Hector gulped. "Sorry."

"Ack!" came a combined cry from the rest of the team, causing Jin to rush over.

"What is it?" he asked as they parted enough to show five very creepy-looking…dogs.

"What the fuck *are* you guys?" rasped Rudy.

They all grimaced, which looked seriously weird on their strange little faces. Jin had never seen anything like them before, and he'd seen a lot of crazy things over the years in the Badlands. Dogs with human faces, though? No, that was a new one.

"We are werecoyotes," the one standing in the front said. "I am Einstein and these are my brothers, Rex, Spot, Rover, and Lightbulb." He then focused on Hector, sniffing the air. "Brother!"

Hector glanced around as everyone looked at him. "Brother? What are you talking about?"

"We share the same father," Einstein explained. "Emiliano mated with our mother many years ago, making us family."

"Ew."

"Man," Alejandro whispered, "I know your dad was a major horndog, but dude…"

"Shut up."

Einstein frowned again. "Anyway, we are here to assist you in your cause. We know about Lord Vestin and his desire to build a zombie army in order to take over the world, and we would like to help stop him from doing that."

He sniffed the air again, this time looking at Jin.

"Unless you've been to the Badlands, I'm not your brother," Jin was quick to point out. "Also, my dad died a long time ago and I'm pretty sure that he never had relations with a coyote even when he was alive."

Einstein's frown deepened further. "I was merely sniffing out who is in charge here."

"Oh, right. Uh…yeah, that's me. I'm the new chief of the San Diego PPD. Jin Kannon."

"Well, Chief Kannon, we may not look like much, but we are excellent at sniffing out crime, spying, and keeping detailed, somewhat copious notes." He sat for a moment and scratched his ear with his hind leg. "In other words, we can be your eyes and ears in the field."

"Can you report through email or something?" asked Rudy, a look of distaste etched upon his face.

"Rudy!" Raina said, slapping the guy on the back of the head before she knelt down and looked across at the coyotes. "Ignore him. He's ignorant, and he should probably remember that he turns into a chicken from time to time."

"ROOSTER!"

"My name is Raina and I'm the deputy of the PPD. As someone who has worked in the area for many years, I would say having your assistance would be a boon to our efforts." She glanced back up at Jin. "Wouldn't you, chief?"

"Hmmm?" He quickly shook himself back to reality. "Oh, yes. Yes! Absolutely. We were just talking about how we needed all the help we could get."

Einstein's frown disappeared instantly. It was replaced by a rather pleasant-looking face, which was almost worse. Jin tried not to say, "Ew" aloud.

"Ew."

He *had* tried.

"Awe, man, really?" Sofia said, pointing at one of the other dogs. It was busily licking its own...well, you know.

"Lightbulb!" Einstein cried out. "How many times have I said not to do that in public?"

"Sorry, boss," Lightbulb replied in a dull voice.

The rest of the dogs were wagging their tails, making it clear they'd thought it was funny that Lightbulb had been called out. It was almost as though the little pack of dogs was a microcosm of Jin and his team of cops.

Did that mean Einstein was playing the role of Jin?
"Ew."

"Agreed, Chief Kannon," Einstein said, clearly having no idea what Jin had actually been thinking. "Agreed."

The little dog then partially morphed, revealing tiny human arms.

"Ew," everyone said, including Raffy, though his actual words were, "Like, ew, man…you know?"

Einstein pulled out a card from the little pack he had around his waist and handed it to Raina. He then zipped the pack back up, morphed again, and gave her a nod.

"If you need anything, that's my contact information."

"Actually," Jin said, forcing himself to get past the way the little monsters looked, "we were just about to go into the city and try to warn people against taking this new drug that Lord Vestin is pushing. We could certainly use the help."

Rudy scoffed. "No way, chief. People aren't going to listen to these…things. They'll run away." Rudy then quickly gave the coyotes a bow and added, "No offense, you monstrous little gremlins, but you're kinda freaky looking."

"All right," Chimi growled, picking up Rudy by his collar. "That's enough. These little guys are cute and you're just too stupid to see it."

It kind of made sense that it was the Cyclops who'd come to their defense in such a way. Raina had, too, of course, but that's just because she was incredibly kind. With Chimi, you could tell she wasn't one who cared about appearances. Rumor had it she was rather attracted to Raffy, by way of example.

"Just ignore them," she said to the coyotes as Rudy struggled to breathe. She dropped him to the ground. "The problem with them is they all think *they* are attractive."

"Ew." That came from the coyotes.

"Exactly." She harrumphed and then shook her head. "But, look, the truth is that you and me are different than them. They can't handle true beauty." She held up an amulet. "I wear this in order to keep my actual appearance hidden from normals. If you'd like, I can have some made for all of you as well." She shrugged. "It *would* make your lives easier."

"I'll be after offerin' to pay for them," stated Lacey, "assumin' they's made where I can no longer see ye as the creepy little rodents ye are."

Chimi put her hands on her hips. "Lacey!"

"Sorry!"

Einstein conferred with his brothers for a moment and then turned back, slowly shaking his head at Chimi. "We appreciate the offer, but we're not ashamed of what we are, and neither should you be, fair lady."

"Ew."

CHAPTER 29

Vestin

*I*t was difficult to watch the training, but it was also necessary. The reason Vestin struggled had nothing to do with the violence, it had to do with the deaths...or was it *true* deaths? Basically, each time one of his zombie soldiers died, Vestin felt a bit of himself go with it. That wasn't because they contained his venom—though, maybe?—it had more to do with the fact that he was losing yet another body in his army.

"Does Emiliano not comprehend that we need to keep our numbers up?" he asked Carina, who was standing beside him.

"He's never been one to care about things like that," she replied. "From his perspective, if you're not good enough to survive during training, you're definitely not good enough to survive when the real thing hits."

It *was* a valid point. Too bad there was a flaw in that logic.

"The problem with his thoughts on the subject, my dear Carina, is that all armies require a certain amount of fodder."

"And probably a mudder, too," she said and then chuckled at her own joke. "You know, fodder and mudder...parents? Ah-hem." She'd clearly recognized Vestin hadn't found it funny. "Sorry. Anyway, I'm not saying Emiliano's strategy is correct. I was just answering your question."

Vestin regarded her for a moment.

Could it have been that Carina and Emiliano shared a fling? Barring that, maybe she'd had a thing for the man back when he *wasn't* a zombie. Vestin could only hope she'd lost that interest, assuming there ever was any, when he was changed because non-zombies relating to zombies in such a physical way would be rather disturbing indeed.

Either way, he wanted to understand where she got her information since it would let him know how open he could be with her regarding his plans.

"Were you two an item or something?"

"No," she replied a little *too* quickly. "I mean, not from his perspective, anyway. He's nothing but an arrogant asshole. At the same time, I've always had a thing for bad boys." She sighed. "I can't help myself. There's just something about a guy who grabs the world by the throat that gets my gears whirring."

Vestin gulped and turned away.

Carina groaned. "Um...no."

He looked back. "Sorry?"

"Look, Vestin—"

"*Lord* Vestin."

"Yeah, right…that. Anyway, I don't know how to tell you this, but the last twenty-seven vampires I've been with pretty much destroyed my interest in vampires as a whole."

His shock was obvious. "Twenty-seven?"

"Not at the same time, Vestin!" She wagged a finger at him. "That's disgusting for you to even think such a thing."

"Wait, what? *I* wasn't assuming you'd been involved in some kind of org—"

"The point I'm trying to make is that in all twenty-seven instances, not a single one of them was a true bad boy, in the sense of the word. In fact, they weren't anything other than douchey *and* arrogant."

He chewed his lip for a moment. "I don't understand the problem."

"Exactly."

Just as Vestin was about to ask for clarification, an arm flew past him, nearly taking his head off.

"Sorry, My Lord," Emiliano called up. "The soldiers are really getting into it now. We'll try to keep the body parts from hitting you."

"Maybe it would be best to keep our ever-dwindling number of soldiers from continuing to dwindle as well, yes?"

Emiliano scrunched up his face for a moment and then he slouched slightly. "Yes, My Lord."

Honestly, at the rate things were going with this army it would be a wonder if Lord Vestin could ever expand his empire from the compound he was standing in. Not that it would be a horrible existence to remain in such a lovely space, but he was destined for more and he knew it. His name was going to be spoken in hushed voices, with people fearing that speaking it too loudly might actually result in him being summoned. People would quake at the mere thought of him stepping into a room where they stood.

Lord Vestin *would* rule the world.

Lord Vestin *would* rule the Netherworld.

Lord Vestin *would* crush all of his foes, subjugating them to his every whim as they begged and pleaded for his mercy.

Another hand flew up, knocking him to the ground and dazing him.

"Lord Vestin will win the day," he said in a slurred voice as he looked up at Carina.

"Right," the witch replied, shaking her head at him mockingly. "You're definitely well on your way to doing that."

CHAPTER 30

Jin

The streets were teeming with people as the Comic-Con convention closed in. Their outfits were pretty amazing, ranging from monsters to science fiction characters to wizards to things that Jin couldn't even describe. One guy was dressed like a blue phone booth.

"I love this time of year," Chimi said, sounding completely chuffed. "The costumes are great!" She kept playing around with the amulet around her neck. "It's the only time of the year when I can actually be myself and normals have no idea. I won first place for best costume two years ago, which was weird, but still very fun."

Jin actually found that to be a somewhat sad story, but he decided not to say anything.

"I am one hundred percent with you, Chimi," said Cano, his eyes locked in on a particular woman who was dancing in the middle of the street. "Look at that lady dressed up like a night elf."

"Gotta love the blue paint," cooed Rudy.

Clive sighed wistfully. "Totally gotta love the blue paint."

Jin wanted to roll his eyes, but he couldn't argue about the blue paint. There was an allure to it. Maybe it served to hide imperfections? That was a shallow thought, obviously, but it didn't make it any less true. He *was* most attracted to the djinn who were completely covered in tattoos, wasn't he? Could that have simply been because he was a djinn himself? And while on that subject, maybe his choice to leave a lot of bare skin on himself was why he wasn't considered more attractive to them.

Probably.

"Keep your eyes to yourself," Sofia warned, smacking Cano on the back of his head.

"Sorry."

Something incredibly interesting caught Jin's eye. It was completely out of place, yet familiar at the same time. Mostly, it concerned him because they already had enough trouble on their plate.

"Um, is it just me, or are those little people zombies?"

"I believe they are," replied Raina as everyone else studied them.

The coyotes stepped forward and began sniffing the air. As one, they started shaking their heads in the negative. Man, those little guys were freaky.

"Nope, they not!" Lightbulb cried out happily. "They's just peoples!"

Einstein agreed. "We've smelled zombies and we've

smelled humans. Those are definitely humans. You can tell because their scent is slightly less rotten."

Slightly?

"They are just small humans who are wearing costumes," said Rex, Rover, and Spot in unison, like they were one entity, though their voices had a sing-song quality and they held the perfect harmony. "Little costumes, one-two-three! Little costumes, you and me!"

Everyone stared at them for a few seconds before turning their eyes to Einstein.

"They've been like that since we were kids," he explained. "Don't ask me to dig into the particulars because I have no idea. All I can say is you should be thankful they didn't break into a full song. That can be super annoy—"

They're low to the street
And they smell like feet
And they like to dress like zombies
Sweet Sweet Sweet!

They're happy as can be
Though they smell like wee
And they love to dress like zombies
Sweet Sweet Sweet!

Zombies, they will go!
Zombies...Yo! Yo! Yo!
Zombies, zombies, zombies,
zombies, zombies...
Say it isn't so!

...and just like that, they stopped and began licking themselves.

"See?" Einstein said. "Half the time you don't even know what the hell they're talking about."

"Okay," Jin said, having to turn the page on his pros/cons list because he'd just run out of room. "Well, let's get down there and start warning people to stay away from *Shaded Past #13*. Raina, you and I will speak with the little zombies. Everyone else, split up and start spreading the word."

Jin waited until everyone had dispersed before confiding in his deputy. He could've just used the connector, but he still preferred hearing an actual voice whenever possible. That was probably not the wisest thing in the world, but he was who he was. Some considered him old-fashioned, and that was probably fair. He was progressive in many things, such as race equality, gender equality, sexuality, and so on, but when it came to things like technology he preferred to avoid it where possible. That wasn't to say he was an idiot about it. There were many medical advances that used technology and he wouldn't sidestep those if he was in need. It was more a case of things like email, texting, and...connectors. Some would argue it brought deeper friendships and better intimacy to their more personal relationships. Jin just happened to disagree.

Regardless, when he could speak using his normal voice, he was going to do so.

"You don't think the coyotes are here as spies for that Vestin guy, do you?"

She gave him a quick glance. "Honestly, I hadn't even considered it until you said something, chief."

"Yeah." He breathed out through his nose as he bit his lower lip. "We're just learning about Vestin, but I'm sure he already knows a lot about us. Sending those little guys along might be a tactic."

"We'll have to keep an eye on them."

Jin nodded at her and then started walking toward the little zombies. They were dead ringers for the zombies they'd battled twice now. Yes, they were one-sixth of the size, but it was still an uncanny resemblance.

"Excuse me," he called out to the one nearest him. "I'm sorry to bother you, but—"

"Awesome outfit, man!" the little guy said. "Going for a John Wayne thing, or more of a Clint Eastwood?"

"Um…I…huh?"

"Looks a little too modern for that, Jim," said another zombie to his right.

"Yeah," Jim said, nodding. "Lyla's right, you don't really fit either dynamic. Who is it you're trying to be?"

"Um...me?"

Raina was studying the little people from all angles, walking around them and everything. They kept looking up at her through their masks, and Jin was certain he'd made out more than one weary frown.

"These are amazing outfits," she said finally. "Did you build them yourselves?"

Lyla raised her hand. "I designed them and Jim helped put them together. We're working on a movie, you see?"

"Exactly right," affirmed Jim. "Always wanted to create a

zombie movie from our perspective and we happened to have won the lottery a few months back. It wasn't quite enough of a win to make a big production, but we've done all right." He raised his hands and spun around. "What better place than the San Diego Comic-Con to pimp the film?" He leaned in slightly. "Honestly, we've completed the filming, but the post-production costs are a lot more than we'd anticipated. There's not nearly enough left from the lottery. Coffers are getting kind of tight, truth be told. With any luck, we'll be able to secure the funding for that here." He squinted. "I don't suppose you're interested in a producer credit?"

"Sorry, no," Jin replied.

Raina shook her head as well.

"Ah, drag. Well, we'll find someone, or maybe a group of people."

"I still think we should run a Kickstarter," Lyla mumbled.

"Yeah, yeah, yeah. I know. But it's just so much work."

"You're just lazy. I said I'd do it."

"Yeah, yeah, yeah."

They looked like they were about to get into a heated discussion and Jin didn't want to be involved with that. He'd already dealt with a lot over the last couple of days—most of which made him reconsider going back to a simpler life of killing people.

"Well," he said, interrupting them, "we're actually from the San Diego—"

Raina interrupted him via the connector, "*You can't tell them we're supers, chief.*"

"*Oh shit. Good point.*"

"San Diego what?" asked Lyla.

"City Security Commission," answered Raina.

"Ah," Lyla said, though she appeared to be seeking her own thoughts on the subject.

"Is there such a thing?"

"As far as you know."

Madison cut in a second later. *"Hey gang, the zombies have all left. I was watching the cartel feeds and I picked up Emiliano telling one of his underlings to bring back all the zombies for military training. Not five minutes later, they were gone. Also, some vampire douche nozzle has arrived at the main* Dogs *compound."*

"That would be Lord Vestin, Mistress," said Rusty.

"Who?"

"He's after bein' the guy in charge of all this zombie shit," Lacey explained.

"Ah, well, he's there now."

"Which would explain the reason Emiliano called them back from the PPD building," Jin mused.

"Well done, Sherlock," said Madison. *"You're really getting the hang of the cop stuff, aren't you?"*

There was only one person laughing through the connector.

"Can it, Rusty," he commanded. Surprisingly, that worked. *"Okay everyone, let's finish up with a few more warnings to people down here and then get back to the precinct. Now that we know what we know, we have to figure out what the hell we're going to do about it."*

"Helllllooooo?" said Lyla, who was waving at them both.

Raina jumped back. "Oh! Sorry!" Raina pointed off

into the distance. "Thought I saw a T-Rex. Love those things."

"Oh yeah, there are a number of them here," said Jim. "They're the best."

"Yeah, they sure are." Raina coughed. "Anyway, we're down here because we heard there are people who are planning to bash zombie costume wearers. We don't know why, and it may be unfounded, but we're just asking anyone wearing these kinds of outfits to be really careful, so watch your backs."

"Wow," said Jim. "Thanks for letting us know!"

"Yeah, no shit," agreed Lyla. "We appreciate it."

"Also," added Jin, "no matter what anyone tells you, stay away from something known as *Shaded Past #13*. That is the most dangerous drug we've seen in a long time."

"Jeez," Jim said, gulping. "I don't do drugs, but we have a few who experiment in our cast. I'll be sure to let them know to stay away."

"Thanks for the heads-up on all this stuff," said Lyla. "You think these events are all simply filled with fun and happiness, but there always seem to be bad seeds hanging around to mess everything up."

"You're absolutely correct," Raina said as she grabbed Jin by the arm and started to pull him away. "Well, we have to keep spreading the word. Please feel free to warn others you run into as well!" She stopped. "Oh, by the way, I'd love to see your movie when it comes out. What's it going to be called?"

As one, Lyla and Jim chorused, *"Anklebiters!"*

CHAPTER 31

Prender

Prender had gone downtown as commanded. He wasn't happy about it, though. His role was to be second-in-command, which he assumed meant he would be leading up the army. No, he wasn't the kind who enjoyed engaging in battles, mostly because he was rather poor at fighting, but he had no issues commanding others to face their doom.

Lord Vestin could do as he wished, however. It wasn't like there was any leverage Prender could use against the man.

Even if he could, would he?

Unlikely.

Prender wasn't great at confrontation. In those moments when he would lie in bed awake well into the night, he often wondered why Lord Vestin had granted him the position in the first place. Had Prender been in Lord Vestin's place, he certainly wouldn't have. That wasn't a self-effacing statement, either. Prender knew his strengths and weaknesses. He was good at organization, design, fashion, and creating a certain pizazz. In other words, being Lord Vestin's personal assistant would have been a much more sensible use for someone like Prender.

But that's not how things went down, and Prender had learned early on that if Lord Vestin was led to believe he'd made a mistake, he would fix it rather quickly. That would be fine had the method most often selected not been murder. You see, Lord Vestin wasn't fond of making mistakes, even though he seemed to do so religiously.

Prender weighed his thoughts for a moment as he gazed down at the various people in their ridiculous costumes.

It was actually a *good* thing that Emiliano had been placed in charge of the army when he really thought about it. If Prender was given the reins, it'd become obvious that Lord Vestin had erred in choosing him for the task. That would be the end of Prender.

Worse, he would've been turned into a zombie.

He shuddered at the thought.

That only lasted a few moments because a slow calm came over his body and mind.

Prender may have been second-in-command in title, though he doubted that would last for very long—but he was no longer expected to handle certain roles. He blinked a few times, feeling a level of exuberance he'd not felt in quite some time. If he played his cards right, he could actually turn his role into something that was perfect for him.

Granted, he would have to be careful in his dealings

with Lord Vestin, but Prender understood his Lord quite well. For one, the man *despised* answering his own phone. Imagine if Prender stepped up and offered to handle that, and many other unworthy things. It could prove to be the perfect arrangement for them both.

He merely needed to determine the most careful way to approach the subject, making it look like Lord Vestin had always been in the right while Prender was the one who had failed.

A humble person would never fall for something like that, of course, but Lord Vestin was miles away from being humble.

Still, one wrong move, and Prender would be peeling off his own skin while waiting to fight in wars.

The stress returned.

Dammit. It was so difficult to know what was going on in the mind of someone like Lord Vestin. Prender knew it all pertained to death and domination, but was there no compassion or leniency toward those who helped him achieve his goals?

Again, unlikely.

Something caught Prender's eye, bringing him back to his purpose for standing on the balcony near the city center. There was a group of people he recognized.

"Isn't that the PPD?" he asked the zombie who was standing in the shadows beside him.

"Yep," it gurgled back. "And *that* is Hector Leibowitz, the current head of the San Diego cartel."

Prender rubbed his chin, thoughtfully. "Interesting."

He watched as the group of people split up, heading in

different directions, but he kept his eyes on the main man who was wearing the cowboy uniform.

"That's their new chief?"

"Yep," replied the zombie. "That's why we originally kidnapped Chief Fysh. Well, I guess she's a Director now. It's tradition for the cartel to kidnap the outgoing chief of the PPD."

"Um-hmmm."

Prender had only half-heard the creature. He was more interested in understanding what the PPD was up to around here. They clearly knew about the circumstances with *Shaded Past #13*, and they'd also learned about Lord Vestin, *and* they knew about the zombies. But why...

"Hmmm," he said, moving from rubbing his chin to tapping it. "I believe they're warning people about our Lord's venom."

"That would be bad."

"It would. Why don't you..." Prender paused and held up a finger upon seeing the new chief speaking to a bunch of small zombies. He pointed. "Do those belong to us?"

"I don't think so," the zombie replied. "They're way too small."

"They are, aren't they?"

"Yep."

Prender felt a devious smile form on his face. His brain danced with potential accolades as an idea struck him so hard it nearly knocked him on his rear end.

"Once they leave, I want you to kidnap one of those little zombies and bring it to the main compound." Prender then spun and put on his best snarl. "And make sure you do not reveal the little cretin to Lord Vestin without my being there or I'll have you dipped in acid and flayed alive."

The zombie gave him a dull look. "Dude, I'm a zombie. Dipping me in acid will hurt, but so what? And being flayed alive is a step up from what I've become. If anything, you'd be doing me a favor."

"Oh."

"Look, Prender," the zombie continued, "I'll get one of those little people and wait for you because you're a decent guy."

Prender blinked a few times. "I am?"

"Yep. In fact, most of the zombies actually appreciate that you don't treat us like pieces of garbage. So if you wouldn't mind sticking with being who you are, we'd appreciate it." He grunted and winced slightly, but forced himself to add, "We already have to deal with Emiliano's bullshit, not to mention Turrrrrd Vestinnnnn…UGH!"

Prender ducked an instant before the zombie's ass exploded.

CHAPTER 32

Jin

 $\mathcal{B}$ y the time they'd returned to the precinct, Madison had configured the main conference area to show the various rooms of each compound. Not all sections of the houses were covered though.

The most interesting visual was of the outside where several zombies were training, and more were pouring in by the minute.

"How did you get that feed?" Jin asked. "We never put any of the cameras outside."

She pressed a button that zoomed the image back in, showing Emiliano's main office. "I was panning around and saw that it was positioned perfectly to look out the big window there." Refocusing it on the army, she added, "I've been keeping an eye on this for a while now. That army is growing pretty damn fast."

"Because of *Shaded Past #13*," Jin grumbled. "Rusty and I saw the first batch of people get turned, and we all spread the word about how dangerous it is to the people attending the conference, but junkies will be junkies and they'll mostly try anything once."

"And that's the problem, Mistress," Rusty added, kneeling before her. "It only takes one dose and you're a zombie."

Jin wasn't a fan of seeing Rusty in his android form kneeling before Madison. It wasn't professional. He knew he'd have to bring it up at some point but now was not the time. They had to focus on the zombies first, then he would worry about office rules, assuming he decided to stay.

In other words, he was probably never going to have that conversation.

"I'm just glad you're here, chief," Raina whispered. "With Director Fysh out of the picture, we could've ended up with someone who wasn't nearly as sensible as you are."

From his perspective, they probably would have gotten someone who actually knew what the hell they were doing. This wasn't his ball of wax. He believed he was working everything fine, but only because he was smart enough to listen to his crew when they spoke. A person who had grown up through the ranks would have been far more effective than he was, though, unless that person was all about bureaucracy. Then it would have been an utter shit show.

Whatever. He was here now; he'd made a commitment, which meant he was going to stick with it until the end.

"This is going to be impossible," said Chimi. "There is

absolutely no way we can do this. His army is growing and it'll start happening even faster with that drug going around. It's going to be massive."

"Is that a reading?" asked Jin, hopefully.

Chimi shook her head. "I don't need to read chicken bones to see that we're in over our heads, chief."

There was a collective groan. If it'd been one of Chimi's infamous readings, according to the team, they would have all felt the battle was actually possible to win. Since she was merely stating what everyone else could see with their own two eyes, however, it only furthered the team's dismay.

"It *does* look bleak," agreed a new voice. They turned to see Director Fysh had come in. "I've been watching the city feeds since our last chat. This is far larger than we can handle." She reached out and put her hand on Hector's. "I'm sorry this is happening so soon into your tenure as the new boss."

That was weird.

Jin knew they'd had a bit of a fling in the past, but she was still PPD and he was still the head of *The Dogs*, as fractured as that was at the moment. It just made for an awkward situation.

Romeo and Juliet, anyone? Sorta, at least. Maybe they were dating again? Not that it was Jin's business, of course, but with Emiliano out of the picture—kind of—it was possible.

What a messed up place Jin had found himself in.

"Well," he said, "since you obviously know there's no chance in hell we're going to be able to beat that army without a bunch more cops to help us through, don't you think we have a special cause for getting more bodies?"

Director Fysh removed her hand from Hector's. "I'm going to do my best to talk with the other Directors and the Executive Directors, of course, because it's clear the zombies are going to take over everything if we don't do something, but I've been through what appeared to be dire straits many times before and they've never stepped up to throw more cops at any of those problems." She gritted her teeth. "My guess is we're going to be on our own here, yet again."

Jin wanted to rage at the stupidity of it all, but to what end? He could bitch and moan for hours and it wouldn't make a damn bit of difference. At some point, they were going to go down fighting. That's just how things like this happened.

He wasn't worried about dying. If he was bitten by some zombie and he felt his blood start to change, he'd simply turn one of his guns on himself and eat a bullet. That had to be better than becoming another member of an undead army bent on destroying the world for some pompous vampire.

What bugged him most was how innocent people were going to be thrust into this nightmare, and after seeing the effects of *Shaded Past #13*, that eventuality appeared to be well underway.

"There's always something like this happening, chief," Raina said, obviously noting his distress.

"Yes, you mentioned that before."

She continued speaking anyway. "Sure, there are times when you could go months, possibly even a year or two before things get crazy. But eventually, some jerk will come along and say, 'We are going to rule the world!' or whatever." She gave him a sad look. "It happens a lot more than you might think."

"She's right," agreed Director Fysh. "If the various precincts pulled cops from all the other precincts every time the world was faced with annihilation, it would simply open the field for more bad actors to start in other places. Then there'd be no chance for us to handle the chaos." She shrugged. "It's why we've always had to figure out a way to handle shit like this on our own." Then, she nodded at the screen. "I've never seen anything *this* bad, though."

"Yeah," agreed Raina. "This is definitely something new."

And that's when it hit Jin. It wasn't an idea he wanted to consider, but if what Director Fysh and Raina were saying was true, it was either that or they all died...or became zombies themselves.

He pointed at the screen as he eyed the crew. "Keep studying that army and see if you can learn their tactics." He then stormed out of the room, tapping Raina and Director Fysh on their shoulders as he left. "I have an idea if you two could give me a few minutes."

They followed him into his office and he shut the door. When he turned back around, he found Director Fysh had taken his chair. For whatever reason, it bothered him a little, but he shook it off and got to explaining.

"I know what I'm about to say sounds absolutely insane, but I really don't see any other option aside from handing in my resignation and wishing you all good luck."

JOHN P. LOGSDON & JENN MITCHELL

"Ouch," said Raina.

He gave her a look. "I wouldn't *actually* do that, Raina." He took off his hat and held it against his chest as he pushed the words from his mouth. "I think I'm going to go talk to Chancellor Frey and see if I can get the Assassin's Guild to come up and help."

Director Fysh laughed as Raina's jaw dropped.

Jin held his composure.

"Wait, you're serious?" Director Fysh asked, losing her smile. "Tell me you're not serious."

"I'm serious." He motioned back toward the conference room with his hat. "You know as well as I do we can't beat the likes of that with our numbers. It's not going to happen."

"Yeah, but..." She stopped and scanned the room, making clear her head was spinning at the thought. "Look, Kannon, that's a big ask. HUGE! First off, can we even afford the cost that comes with something like this? I've never hired a professional assassin before, but I'm guessing the answer is no. And even if we could afford it, getting the clearance for them to come topside is going to be damn near impossible."

"But *not* impossible?"

Director Fysh gave him a look. "I don't believe anything is utterly impossible, Chief Kannon, but it'll be a fucking miracle."

Jin nodded. "Then it seems both of us have some massive hills to climb. Leave the negotiation regarding the cost to me. I have a few ideas on that front." He hoped his plans would work, but only time would tell. "It could very well be that I can't get them to agree to come up here even if you do get the clearance, but dammit we have to try something or this Lord Vestin asshole is going to take over the entire damned city!"

"And he's not going to stop there," Director Fysh agreed.

"Nope." Jin put his hat back on. "As for getting clearance, I think we both know that's above my pay grade, so hopefully you can convince the powers that be on that front."

She slammed her hands on the desk. "Fine, I'll get the clearance if you can get the assassins. If either of us fails… well…"

"Let's not think that way," Raina chimed in. "I believe in you guys, and I believe in our team." She quickly looked down at her datapad. "On top of that, there's a full moon due soon. If nothing else, the zombies are going to have their hands full dealing with me during my cycle."

Jin wasn't sure how to respond to that, but he felt the hairs on his neck stand up when Director Fysh rasped, "Yikes."

CHAPTER 33

Vestin

*A*fter taking an hour-long tour of the building and the compound, they entered the main office and Vestin walked behind the big desk and took the chair. It wasn't exactly a throne, but simply seeing the look on Emiliano's face at having to stand on the other side of the desk the man had assuredly claimed as his own for years was priceless.

"It will do, I suppose," he said in an uppity voice as he studied the room with a measure of distaste. "At some point, I shall require something more befitting a ruler of my stature, but in due time."

Lord Vestin thought he heard the sound of something whirring above him. Looking up, he could see nothing but a small shadowy area near the ceiling. It was strange, yet something in his mind assured him it was nothing to worry about.

The concern immediately vanished when Prender

strolled into the room with one of the zombie soldiers. With them was a miniature version of the zombie himself.

"What is this?" Vestin demanded. "Did I not command you to keep watch over the city while we prepared the army for attack?"

"You did, My Lord," Prender replied, "but I felt you would want to know about this immediately." He gestured at the small zombie as he spoke.

"A zombie teddybear?" Vestin shook his head and pinched the bridge of his nose. "I'll admit it's adorable, Prender, but what am I supposed to do with it?"

"I'm *not* a teddy bear, you shit-squeezing vulva!"

Lord Vestin leaned forward. "Have you somehow managed to shrink Janet Smith?" He regarded Prender again. "If so, I believe I have undervalued your...well... value!"

"Um, no, My Lord. This is an actual person. Her name is Etna and she's playing a part in a movie called *Anusbusters.*"

"It's *Anklebiters,* you fucking goat scrotum. Now, let me go!"

Vestin sat back again, weighing things.

He was sure there was a valid reason for Prender to bring this little person to his compound. Granted, there *was* the costume, which looked very much like his real zombies, but..." His head snapped up. "Are you suggesting that we turn all of these little people into child soldiers?"

"What? No!" Prender quickly relaxed. "Sorry. No, My Lord. I'm suggesting that if our zombies were this size, yet somehow retained their power..."

"Oh my!" Lord Vestin stood straight up and put his

hands on the desk. His face was filled with enlightenment. "Prender, you've outdone yourself." He then pointed at Carina. "I know your first task, my witch."

"Let me guess," she replied dully, "you want me to turn our army into a bunch of dwarves?"

"What?" Emiliano yelped, as did the zombie who had worked with Prender to bring in the little actor.

"I do not want anything of the kind," Vestin said, appearing more than mildly disappointed.

"Oh."

"Thank goodness," replied Emiliano.

"You're telling me," agreed the other zombie.

"What I want you to do, Carina," Vestin pressed on, "is *not* to turn our zombies into dwarves, but to turn them into little zombies."

Carina frowned at him and raised an eyebrow. "Riiight."

As for Emiliano and the other zombie, they both groaned, "Shit."

CHAPTER 34

Jin

*J*in hadn't wanted to bring the team in on his plan until he'd gotten the go-ahead from Director Fysh. He just didn't feel it would be fair to do something like that. Getting people's hopes up merely to dash them was cruel. Then again, it could very well be that Jin was going to fail horribly in his attempt to get the Assassin's Guild to help at all. And even if he could, what was the likelihood that Director Fysh could get approval to bring them all topside? There was a possibility that Chancellor Frey may have some pull in that area since she carried a lot of dirt on people from all walks of life. The question was whether or not she'd use it.

He kept his eye on the screen in the back as his team found their desks.

The army of zombies was vast and it was going to get bigger fast. That *Shaded Past #13* drug, or whatever it was,

JOHN P. LOGSDON & JENN MITCHELL

had knocked those people on their asses quickly, and they were turning into zombies in less than a minute. Something that effective would spread like an untamed virus. On top of that, there was a vampire running the show, which could only mean he'd somehow figured out how to mass-produce his own venom.

"Wait," he said, raising a hand to silence everyone as dread filled his mind. "Um...is it just me or do we effectively have a vampire who has somehow figured out a way to make his venom work on supers?"

"Shiiiiit," said Rudy as a couple of feathers sprouted out of his neck. He pulled them free. "Sorry, that happens when I get sufficiently freaked out."

Director Fysh's face made clear she would have sprouted feathers, too, if she'd been capable of doing so.

Jin wasn't feeling much differently.

"Okay," the Director said, "*that's* going to give me leverage."

"I'll say," Jin replied, gulping. "I'd argue it'll give me some, too." He turned back to the team, who were all babbling back and forth. "Listen up, gang! I know this is wigging us all out and there's not a person here who doesn't recognize this is some next-level trouble the world has never seen, but I have a plan."

"Uh oh," said Chimi. He gave her a look. "Sorry, chief, it's just whenever I say 'I have a plan,' people tend to reply with 'uh oh,' so I just assumed..." She sniffed. "Never mind. You were saying?"

He held his frown for a few moments more before letting it go. "I was saying that there's a possible way to get the help we need in order to clear up this problem of ours, but it's not a guarantee." He went to reach for his hat but stopped himself. "I'm going to go and speak with the Assassin's Guild."

"Whoa, what?" said Clive.

"I'm with Horse Boy," Lacey blurted. "Yer plannin' to do what now?"

Clive grimaced. "Hey!"

"I can't think of a group of people who are more qualified to get in and destroy this army we're looking at here." Jin looked again at the monitors, swearing he'd seen the top of a zombie's head come into the frame for a moment. Maybe he was in the office? "Anyway, unless one of you has a better plan, like maybe the creation of another twenty-five androids or something, I'm all ears."

Rudy's hand shot up.

"Before you suggest another twenty-five androids, Rudy," Jin said, glancing at him from the corner of his eyes, "just know that's not going to happen."

Rudy's hand went back down.

He understood their reluctance, but there weren't many options here. Actually, he could think of none, aside from what he'd suggested, and even that was admittedly a long shot.

"Rusty, you'll be joining me," Jin declared, thinking it might be the wisest move since otherwise the android would merely stand around fawning over Madison, and she had a lot of work to do. He nodded at Raina. "Deputy Mistique will be running the show while I'm gone. What she says goes." She stood up a little taller at that. Good. "Raffy and Petey, we would appreciate any help you can provide Madison on building out weapons or whatever else you can think of." Jin then turned his attention to Hector. "If you and your crew are willing, we could really use some more people out in the neighborhoods warning people about that *Shaded Past #13* drug. I'll admit I don't know a lot about your cartel, but if it's anything like I've seen over my years in the Badlands, I would imagine you're more in tune with the people than the police are."

Hector and his *Dogs* glanced at each other and tilted their heads back and forth. Were they communicating in some weird werewolf way that Jin had never known about? Maybe they had their own connector technology?

"It's probably true," Hector admitted, cutting off Jin's thoughts.

"Right."

They all just stood there staring at him, making him think he was supposed to say something else. What, though? He'd already made clear what he was expecting of them, so what could he have possibly added? Thinking of some of the books he'd read about the topside, he could have said, "Long live the queen" or something, but he recalled there was no queen of the United States. Instead, he just said, "Um...go get em!"

It seemed to work since everyone got moving.

Director Fysh stepped up next to him. "You're a natural at this, chief, though I'm not sure why you want to bring Rusty with you. It would probably be wiser to bring a different officer, or, frankly, to go alone."

"You do remember that prior to being turned into an android, Rusty was altered to be Madison's slave, right?"

"Ah. Right." She pointed at him. "Wise decision."

"Thanks."

CHAPTER 35

Vestin

*L*ord Vestin stepped up to the main pulpit at the head of the army and looked down at his new dwarven empire of zombies. It was rather less than impressive when compared to their original seven-and-a-half-foot tall bodies, but he knew their strength was intense. He hoped that would be the case, at least.

Glancing over at Emiliano, he understood the zombie was completely unhappy with his new height.

Too bad.

This wasn't about him, nor was it about anyone in the army. They were soldiers. Nothing more; nothing less.

The added benefit was how they'd all been moved to a large chamber in the bowels of the main building. While Vestin preferred the outdoors, he wanted to make sure he could speak without fear of anyone spying. He held no qualms about the PPD watching his army training, of course. If anything, that would only serve to terrify the police even further. But his words were sacred, to his way of thinking. They belonged to him and his minions only.

Besides, there was something fitting about having a dark, cathedral-like setting for these kinds of speeches.

"Hear my words," he bellowed as all their faces looked up at him. "We are on the precipice of greatness!" He would've preferred to specifically note that only *he* was on the precipice of greatness, but sometimes Vestin had to play the role as it was given. "Soon, the world will grovel at my...our feet! I...we will rule over them with an iron finger!"

"Thumb," Prender whispered.

"Hmmm?"

"It's iron thumb, My Lord."

Lord Vestin merely glared at him momentarily before turning his attention back to the mass of zombies.

"Once I...we have taken over San Diego..." He stopped.

This was make-or-break time. Playing some foolish game where he included his servants in the glory was ridiculous. It was time to throw caution to the wind and point out how this *was* all about him.

"*I* will turn my attention to neighboring cities. Each of you will fight, crush, and die—if necessary—in order to aid me in building *my*...yes, you heard that right, *MY* empire!"

At that point, it was clear even to Vestin that he simply wasn't the sharing type.

"After you have spread my venom throughout the

topside, you will infest the Netherworld, claiming it under my throne as well." His smile almost hurt as the muscles strained to stretch beyond their normal proportions. "Soon, my little minions, not a single person shall exist who does so outside of my rule."

They were dead silent, and that was fine. Yes, cheering would have been wonderful, but he hadn't truly expected his zombies to do so.

A hand went up near the front.

That was odd.

He blinked at her a few times. "Yes?"

"Um…sorry to ask, My Lord," the woman said, "but originally you were talking like it was all about 'us,' yes? Like this was kind of a collective thing? Then you started down it being all about 'you,' right? More singular? Like a somewhat selfish thing."

"Yes? Do you have a question?"

"Oh, well, I was just wondering if we have any role to play in this other than fighting, crushing, and…" She leaned over to the person next to her. "What was the other thing he said?"

"Dying."

"Oh, right." She looked back up at Lord Vestin. "Fighting, crushing, and dying. Is there going to be more to our existence than that?"

"What more do you need?" he asked. "Is it not good enough that you are serving my wishes?"

"I mean, I guess," she said, though she didn't seem convinced. "I'm just thinking it'd be nice to have more of an existence than merely killing people, you know?

Maybe a hobby or something?" She grabbed her belly. "Don't get me wrong, it's not that I think serving you is beneath me or anythiiiiiiiing—" The jet stream of shit that blasted the zombie behind her begged to differ. She spun around and said, "Sorry. I just...um...well, sorry."

The guy wiped his face clean but otherwise didn't seem all that bothered. He *was* a zombie, after all.

Vestin actually imagined at that moment that he could simply close down the entire program and move on with his life. Honestly, there were plenty of topside government jobs where he could impose tons of pain and anguish on people, lording over them and their daily lives, forcing them to stand in ridiculously long lines and fill out pointless reams of paperwork. No, it wasn't quite the same as ruling the world, but not having to deal with the "feelings" of his army would be a huge plus.

Kingdom versus fiefdom...each had its plusses and minuses.

One thing was for sure, if he could do the entire venom thing over again, he would've focused more of his efforts on making them *only* find happiness in serving his needs.

It was too late for that, unfortunately.

"I'll tell you what," he said, trying his best to sound believable, "each of you who serves above and beyond the call of duty, shall be rewarded in ways you can't even imagine." He wasn't lying. His plan was to kill them all in horrific ways and then replace them with better versions once he'd settled into his new kingdom. "How does that sound? Better?"

Their heads nodded collectively.

"Excellent. Swell. Wonderful. Terrific." He was fighting against sounding sarcastic, but it wasn't easy. "Again, ruling the world is the goal, my minions. Keep that as your primary focus and you have my word that you'll most assuredly get what's coming to you!"

That time, miraculously, they cheered.

CHAPTER 36

Jin

*B*efore leaving to head back to the Badlands, Jin went out to the beach in order to think things through. He'd again missed the sunset, which was a bit of a letdown, but at least the water was comforting.

Sadly, not much else was. He wasn't sure about his plan, for one, but he also couldn't think of anything else that might work. His crew on the PPD were solid or seemed to be. They showed up for work, anyway. Plus, they *did* seem to care about the community and the city itself. Maybe that was imposed upon them during their own Integration cycles, but even if that were the case…so what? The fact that they cared was all that mattered to Jin.

Rusty was going to be a challenge. There was no doubt about that. The good news was the guy had some massive power at his disposal, and he could *not* be turned into a zombie. Honestly, if they'd had twenty-five Rustys, as Rudy had suggested, they probably *would* be able to get everything back under control. Based on the discussions he'd had with Raina and Director Fysh, however, the cost alone would be prohibitive.

It amazed Jin how people would pay exorbitant amounts of money for some things while considering other items—more important items—worth so much less.

Too bad that was the world they lived in.

"Back in my spot again, eh?" Madison called out as she walked up next to him and looked out at the ocean.

"Sorry."

"I'm joking. You're fine." She took in a deep breath of the ocean air. "I love that smell."

"Fish?"

"Yep, and the salty air." Madison kept looking forward, but asked, "Do you really think the assassins will help us out?"

"No idea, but I don't see any other options. Do you?"

"Never even saw that one as an option, so nope."

"Yeah."

She walked out in front of him and turned around, looking up into his eyes. It wasn't a seductive look, thankfully. Jin wasn't in the mood for that right now, although her level of perfection was clearly capable of remedying his current lack of libido.

"You're bringing Rusty? Why?"

"I think you know."

Madison smirked. "It's probably for the best, considering the circumstances."

"It's probably for the best," he agreed, "but mostly because it's better for him."

"You disapprove of our situation?" She laughed at that. "Jealousy, maybe?"

Jin liked Madison. He truly did. The problem was he didn't like what she'd done to Rusty. It hadn't bothered him much at first before Rusty had become an android, but seeing him act the way he did while in a human-like body changed Jin's perspective.

Maybe it shouldn't have taken that level of visualization, but it did.

"Not in the least, Madison," he replied, trying to be gentle. "I don't believe in jealousy. But, if I'm being honest, I also don't believe in forcing someone to live under your complete control."

That caused Madison to cross her arms. Jin hadn't meant it as a full-on attack. Or did he?

"I suppose that's up to him, isn't it?" she challenged.

"I don't know, is it?" he asked seriously. "You're the one who coded his particulars, so does he actually have any choice in the matter?"

She merely glared.

Jin shook his head. "Look, I'm not judging you for being who you are."

"It kinda feels like exactly what you're doing."

"Well, it's not. It's just that Rusty could be a decent guy if you'd let him. Hell, you may even find he worships you simply because he actually *wants* to. Would that be so horrible?" She said nothing. "As it stands, he doesn't really have a choice, which, if I'm being honest, is beneath you."

Her eyes grew somewhat cold.

"I think I'll leave you to your thinking tonight, *Chief* Kannon."

233

With that, she walked away, leaving him there to stare at the ocean alone.

"Shit," he hissed to himself.

It was just one thing after another in this damned place. He hadn't wanted to get into a fight with Madison, but he also wasn't wrong with what he'd said. Hopefully, after she cooled off a bit, she'd see that, too.

Probably not.

Regardless, Madison was messing with Rusty's head, or already *had* messed with his head, and Jin wasn't a fan of that. If Jin had just been some guy, he wouldn't have said a word, but he was the chief here and Rusty was one of his officers. That meant something to him. Besides, if Rusty had entered into some kind of contract with her in a willing way, it would've been fine and dandy. Jin would've kept his yap shut, after telling them to keep it professional while at work, and moved on as if everything was normal.

That wasn't the case, though, and Jin's job didn't stop with merely helping to keep the law, in his estimation anyway. He was there to guide and assist his crew wherever possible, to help them grow into better officers and people.

Man, he was *not* qualified for this job.

Or maybe the Integration had changed him enough so that he was? He clearly cared enough about Rusty to fight for the guy, right? That had to mean something.

It meant something to Jin, and that's all that mattered at the moment.

Speaking of Rusty, everyone knew he had a thing for Madison. He was programmed to. It wasn't even an attempted secret in the precinct. As a matter of fact, Jin recalled learning about it within the first five minutes of speaking with the team.

And that's why Rusty was finding it difficult to work with Jin.

It was simple math. A new guy shows up, holds a position of power in the precinct, and has a heartfelt conversation with a woman Rusty worships, and suddenly the AI feels threatened that he may lose her. It was a classic jealousy situation that Jin had read contracts about over his years as an assassin. He never took any of those contracts because he knew better than to deal with things like jealousy. It was unhealthy for the person taking out the contract, and even more unhealthy for the person they'd taken the contract out on.

There was a sound off to his left, about forty-five degrees behind him. He reached out with his magic but found no discernible heartbeat. That could mean only one thing.

"Rusty," he said in a calm voice, "is that you?"

The android stepped out of the shadows, walking out to stand by Jin.

"How'd you know?"

"I have my ways," he stated, but then pushed right to the heart of the matter at hand, knowing it was going to be a rocky conversation. "That doesn't matter. What does is that I think you've been treated unfairly by Madison."

"Watch your words, skin man," Rusty growled. "I can shred you faster than you reach for those fancy guns of yours."

Under normal circumstances, Jin had the feeling his

nuts would be flying toward the horizon right about now, but something told him Rusty's programming wouldn't actually allow him to do anything because Jin was the chief...*his* chief.

He wasn't going to say that, though. Instead, he would continue using a relaxed voice and show genuine caring.

"I understand you're upset," Jin began, "but I want you to do a quick scan of the internet and let me know if there are any instances where jealousy turns out to be a good thing." He quickly held up a finger. "Let me rephrase that. Are there any instances where jealousy was a good thing for all parties involved?"

Rusty's eyes glazed over for a few seconds. "No."

"No. And do you know why that is?"

The android shook his head.

"It's because jealousy is something whereby the person who is jealous thinks of another person as their own property." He pulled his glasses down slightly. "Do you think of Madison as your property?"

"No!" It was more of a rasp than a bellow. "I'm *her* property."

"Then how is it that you're jealous of what your owner thinks or does?"

"I...uh..."

Jin was worried the guy might literally overheat.

"Look, Rusty, the reason I said Madison has been unfair to you is because she's not allowed you to experience life outside of your singular devotion to her. She's programmed you that way, right?" Rusty didn't answer. "I'm guessing she did. Worshiping every step she takes isn't a choice you've made; it's a choice she's made for you. On top of that, I'm assuming she's even encoded this jealousy so you'd feel further frustration when you think of her being with someone else." Jin let that sink in for a few seconds. "At the same time, you probably believe you love her, but I'll ask you to look up whether or not love is freely given or programmatically forced, and what do you think you'll find?"

Rusty's eyes dulled again and then he looked dismayed. "It should be freely given."

"Do you feel you've been allowed that option?"

"No." His voice was barely audible. "But I can't help how I feel because it's part of my programming."

Jin wasn't sure how these things worked, but he asked, "Are you capable of adjusting your own programming?"

"I can, yeah." He looked around as if searching for something. "You think I should?"

"I think you shouldn't love someone simply because you've been created to love someone. If you genuinely love Madison, you'll know; if not, that's okay too. It doesn't mean you can't still be friends." He reached out and patted Rusty's arm. "I'll be honest, aside from family, I've never been in love." He dropped his hand and reached up to rub the rim of his hat. "In other words, I have no idea what it actually feels like. From what I've witnessed, however, true love isn't loaded with jealousy. So, my advice would be to rip out the forced love code and start evaluating your feelings for Madison again. If you still find you love her, and you still want to worship her, at least it will be freely given."

Rusty was nodding, his mouth slightly hanging open. It was so human that Jin was almost beside himself with amazement. Honestly, had he not known Rusty was all wires and circuits under his "skin," Jin would have believed he was just another dude.

"You're right, chief," he said. "I'm sorry I was a dick. I—"

"You don't need to apologize. We're good." Jin looked back out at the ocean. "I know I've said you're coming with me to the Badlands, and I *do* think it would be good if you did, but I'm going to give you the option to back out if you want. I've just laid a lot on you, so I'll understand if you want to take a day to think things through instead." After a few more wave crashes, he asked, "Do you want to stay back or do you think you'll be able to handle that kind of pressure right now? Again, it's completely your call and I won't think anything less of you if you need the time."

Rusty nodded slowly. "No, I'll go. I'll be fine."

"I'm glad." Jin breathed in the fishy, salty air. "We'll leave first thing in the morning."

"Okay."

The sound of the ocean brought Jin a measure of peace. The day had been incredibly stressful and having conversations like the one he'd just shared with Madison and then with Rusty hadn't helped at all.

The ocean, though…it was like music to his soul.

"Listen, Rusty," he said, "if you need to talk more about this stuff, just know I'll be there for you."

"Really?" Rusty sounded flabbergasted.

"Of course."

"Jeez, chief, I totally misjudged you. I mean, just five minutes ago I was planning to rip your heart out, split it in two, shove one piece down your throat and the other piece up your ass, and then as you squirmed and choked I was going to punch you in the spine so it would be severed in two." He held a momentary look of relief. "Man, I'm glad I didn't actually do that."

"Me too, Rusty," Jin replied, his throat suddenly dry. "Me, too."

~

THE END

~

Thanks for Reading

If you enjoyed this book, would you **please leave a review** at the site you purchased it from? It doesn't have to be a book report... just a line or two would be fantastic and it would really help us out!

John P. Logsdon
www.JohnPLogsdon.com

John was raised in the MD/VA/DC area. Growing up, John had a steady interest in writing stories, playing music, and tinkering with computers. He spent over 20 years working in the video games industry where he acted as designer, programmer, and producer on many online games. He's now a full-time comedy author focusing on urban fantasy, science fiction, fantasy, Arthurian, and GameLit. His books are racy, crazy, contain adult themes and language, are filled with innuendo, and are loaded with snark. His motto is that he writes stories for mature adults who harbor seriously immature thoughts.

Jenn Mitchell

Jenn Mitchell writes humorous Urban Fantasy from the heart of South Central Pennsylvania's Amish Country. When she's not writing, she enjoys traveling, crafting, cooking, hoarding cookbooks, and spending time with the World's most patient and loving significant other. She also writes Cozy Mysteries as J Lee Mitchell.

CRIMSON MYTH PRESS

Crimson Myth Press offers more books by this author as well as books from a few other hand-picked authors. From science fiction & fantasy to adventure & mystery, we bring the best stories around!

www.CrimsonMyth.com